OCEAN OF LARD

Subhumanoid Breakdancers Can't Stop Reading
Choose Your Own Mind-Fuck Fests!

"Just like the Choose Your Own Adventure books I used to read as a kid, but full of perverted sex and gore!"
        - Kara, age 27

"You get to see the characters die over and over again, in many different ways!"
        - Tony, age 22

"Why read when you can pretend it's a video game?"
        - Intricate Cunt, age 19

"This series should be called: 'Make An Attempt To Choose Your Own Path In An Adventure Fucked To The Extreme, But Realize That Your Choice Has No Effect On The Story. Jerk Off And Cry Yourself To Sleep Feeling Useless, Alone, and Empty.'"
        - Fetalrust, age 17

"I bought a sex doll. I fucked it three times in about an hour. It was great!"
        - Albie, age 31

CHOOSE YOUR OWN MIND-FUCK FEST

OCEAN OF LARD

by Kevin L. Donihe and Carlton Mellick III

Illustrated by Terrasa Ulm

ERASERHEAD PRESS

PORTLAND, OR

ERASERHEAD PRESS
205 NE BRYANT
PORTLAND, OR 97211

ISBN: 0-9762498-2-0

WWW.ERASERHEADPRESS.COM

Printed in the USA.

AUTHOR'S NOTE

This is a parody of one of those kickass *Choose Your Own Adventure* books that you used to read as a kid to avoid those crappy *Hardy Boys* books. We were going to originally call the series *Choose Your Own Fucked Up Adventures* but wimped out at the last minute for obvious reasons. Normally I wouldn't be too concerned about this kind of thing but I had other people involved and I didn't want them to get screwed. We went with *Mind-Fuck Fest* because it was extremely lame and parodies of brand names have been traditionally lame throughout history. Still, it gets the point across and uses the word *fuck*. And let me tell you, using *fuck* in your book title is so edgy and punk rock that even that guy with the mosh pit tattooed on his asshole will be envious for at least 20 minutes.

Fraggle attack!

Anyway, a few years back a lot of the Eraserhead Authors used to gather in the absurdist.cc chatroom to discuss ways to take over the literary world, discuss our favorite books and the arts, and bullshit about walrus porn, Tony Micelli, pickled meat products, and other random nonsense. Kevin L. Donihe and I, the two unemployed people who spent most of our sundays chatting even if we were the only two people there, also got into brainstorming ideas for books together. It turned out that both of us were tinkering around with similar ideas. One idea was to write an entire book in a fake language, which I ended up doing with *Fishy-fleshed*. And another idea was to write a screwed up Choose Your Own Adventure for adults. Months later we decided to join forces for a CYOA project. We agreed on the pirate theme and used my title *Ocean of Lard*, which was the title of a song I wrote in high school.

If you are unfamiliar with the work of Kevin L. Donihe, you are in for a treat. This guy is an insanely brilliant (or brilliantly insane) author who writes some weird and hilarious shit, and his crazy persona is much like that of a young Hunter S. Thompson on crack. If you like his section of this book make sure to read more of his novels. He's got a ton of them coming out in the near future.

Anyway, hope you enjoy it.

- Carlton Mellick III, 3/2/05 7:13 pm

You shouldn't have molested all those children.

But you couldn't stop yourself, you couldn't fight the voices in the back of your head. And that old fisherman saw you naked with little Angie out by the creek, slithering off her strawberry panties and pinning her tiny pink tongue against the side of her mouth. Now you have to run. Get out of the country before the police catch up with you.

You curse at yourself and stab your thigh with a toenail clipper.

Screaming *sick, sick, sick* at your reflection in the mirror.

Driving all day, nonstop, until your brown van runs out of gas. Then you step out and continue on foot.

Just after blisters begin to form on your heels, you notice there isn't more highway up ahead. The road just ends.

Upon closer inspection, you see the four-lane interstate continues as a small hiking trail. And next to it a sign made of wood scraps and barbed wire with four words carved into it:

A town? Out there?

The landscape is barren. Nothing for miles in every direction. If there's a town out there, it is most likely just a couple burned down farms.

But a small deserted town is just the type of place you're looking for. The more isolated the better. So you shake the pain off of your blisters and take the path.

Near twilight, you hear seagulls and strange splashing sounds. The sounds of the ocean.

"In the middle of Wyoming?" you ask yourself.

A greasy smell hangs in the air. It seems as if you're going towards a slaughterhouse or maybe some kind of chemical plant.

After passing through some jagged hills, you come to a clearing. There aren't any signs of industry or buildings. Just an enormous landscape of white and gray sand that stretches into the horizon.

But wait . . .

The sand is moving.

It isn't a clearing at all. It is some kind of giant lake of white fluid. You step closer and find yourself on a beach of charcoal sand. The greasy smell grows stronger. It smells like somebody cooking bacon. There are seagulls flying overhead that look like they are made out of ground beef. And there are these crabs/jellyfish crawling in the sand by your feet making bubble-click noises and trying to pinch your toes.

It is more like a seashore than a lake. You look out at the strange liquid. Enormous white waves curl towards the beach, roaring at you. These waves move more like pudding than water. No, something even thicker than pudding. It reminds you of the blob.

The meaty seagulls scatter when a wave splats against the sand, squawking and trying not to get stuck in the smelly goop.

You move in to touch the liquid.

"Watch out for those creeper waves," a squirmy voice says from behind.

You turn to see a crispy hobo sitting among some rocks.

"What is this?" you ask the hobo.

"Haven't you seen the ocean before?" he responds, rubbing charcoal sand off of his thighs.

"What is it made out of?" you ask the hobo. "How big is it?"

"You're annoying," says the hobo. "Don't talk to me."

And the hobo stands from the rocks and begins to walk away from you.

"Wait," you call out to the filthy man. "Which way to Pirate Town?"

The hobo waves his hand in the opposite direction and continues on.

You arrive to a small town of splintery huts and filthy drunkards. The people are blackened and oily, moving like insects. But all are pirate-like in some way. Dressed up like Black Beards, Long John Silvers, Captain Morgans, and Calico Jacks. One snatches a resting seagull from a fencepost and crushes it beneath yellow teeth. Another vomits white gunk in an alleyway. It looks like the stuff from the sea.

You don't bother them.

Near the docks, you see a sign that reads:

Navigator Wanted for The Rotten Sore
Cabin Boy Wanted for The Eye World

You see these two ships in the dock:

THE ROTTEN SORE

Twice as large as any pirate ship you've seen, the vessel waits in the harbor, shimmering. Foot long spikes jut from knotted, wormy wood. Tattered leather comprises sails bedecked in chains and covered with random graffiti. A black and red anarchy flag flies defiant over a lookout nest. Further down, you notice a plank. It juts from the left hand side of the ship like a tongue. Perhaps it is a tongue.

THE EYE WORLD

From a distance, this ship resembles a black skyscraper, thirty stories tall and wide. But upon closer inspection, you see that it is some kind of sailing vessel. An enormous metal cube that seems to have been put together like a patchwork quilt. Several different types of metal welded together. In some places, the metal is rusting, or coated in tar or algae. About halfway up the side of the ship, the metal patchwork becomes a chaotic maze of circuitry and wires. You don't see any of the ship's crew, or any sign that life exists on the ship at all. But you can feel the vibration of electricity as it pulses out of the ship and across the landscape.

You contemplate taking a job on one of the ships. The police will never find you out there. It is the safest place you're likely to ever find. But you don't know the first thing about sailing and it's likely to be dangerous.

If you want to board The Eye World, turn to page 21.
If you want to board The Rotten Sore, turn to page 22.
If you'd like to stay in Pirate Town, turn to page 36.

You don't want to get into any more trouble so you tell Frog Girl she better go to the helm.

"You're no fun," she says, blowing her long tongue at you.

After she leaves and you jerk off, you try to put on your new outfit. The leather underwear seems to be made for a teenaged girl. You force it on, but it is far too tight. It squishes your testicles when you walk. So you wear your old clothes, disobeying the Captain and dreading what she will do to you once she finds out.

You decide to explore the torture dungeon. There doesn't seem to be more than one exit. The door is locked. You follow the walls into the shadowy side of the room and discover a thin hallway. There is very little light, but you can make out several doors. Perhaps you can find a room to hide in.

"Where do you think you're going?" a deep voice calls from behind.

You turn around to see Lox, the walrus/man, completely naked and holding a flog.

"Those rooms are off-limits," he says. "Lie on the table."

The flabby creature approaches you with an enormous elephant erection, wrinkled and puffy, slapping against his thighs as he walks.

You can't stop yourself from running. Darting down the thin hall and breaking through one of the doors. Charging into darkness. Your knees slam into something hard and you tumble over it. Your chin breaks against a gravel ground.

Gripping your legs and blood dripping down your neck, you stay hidden behind a block of some kind.

You hear Lox in the hallway, going from door to door and moaning at you to come out.

Once your eyes adjust to the darkness you can tell you are in some kind of storage holding tons of appliances, like refrigerators, stoves, blenders. And there is movement all around you. Monstrous shadows spidering out of the corners.

Lox opens the door and screams, "If you're in here, get out now! You don't underst—"

His voice is cut off by claws ripping into his belly. They are human-shaped creatures with rotten drippy flesh, eating the intestines out of the flailing walrus/man who can't get himself to scream. He drops to the floor and blubber-quakes as they scoop out the contents of his torso. His enormous penis ejaculating as they eat him.

There are shrilling gasps behind your ears and thick fluids pooling onto your shoulder.

You don't even get to scream before your throat is ripped out.

THE END

You're tired. The last thing you need is more stimulation. But Salvatore/Timmy is so adamant. So eager. And he seems good-natured enough. You don't fear or dread him like most other pirates. Besides, he's aroused your curiosity.

"Are ye going to get up or what?"

You nod. "Yeah, just give me a second."

Salvatore/Timmy stands with his arms crossed over his chest. He taps his foot as you attempt to shake away bleariness. Whatever he wants you to see must be really important.

Or really fun.

You get up. Legs wobble as you walk towards Salvatore/Timmy. He drapes his arm around your shoulder and escorts you out on deck.

The moon is bright and full. You see everything clearly. *Anarchy in the UK* playing strings glisten. Wooden boards appear slick and golden. Past the still-harbored ship, sand looks almost as white as the ocean that stretches out like whipped crème infinity.

The sight is strangely majestic.

You turn to Salvatore/Timmy. "Where are we going?"

"To the gunwall on the starboard side."

You have no idea what 'gunwalls' are, but figure you'll find out soon enough.

You walk across the length of the ship and stop at the far edge. You look down. Lard waves splash *The Rotten Sore*'s hull. They make a syrupy sucking sound. The ship moves back and forth, rocking on these gentle currents of fat. Then you hear something behind you. It sounds like wheels in motion. You turn toward the noise.

An old wheelchair-bound pirate moves with the rocking of the ship, back and forth, back and forth. His tongue lolls. His eyes stare without blinking.

"Who's that?"

"That's Squirrelly Pete. He's here for the fun, too."

"But he looks comatose."

"Aye, that he is. Guess someone forgot to take him in, but

that's no reason he can't join us."

You nod. It sounds reasonable.

"Let me call the merflids now."

Merflids?

Salvatore/Timmy unleashes a low, throaty bellow. It sounds like a mix between a bird, a walrus, and a blender.

"What the hell are you doing?"

"Calling merflids, of course."

You turn back to the ocean. Something is rising to the surface. Large bubbles appear in the lard.

Salvatore/Timmy smiles. "Seems I've attracted one!"

The bubbles increase in number. You wonder what a merflid might be. A sea-monster? A mermaid-thing?

Your questions are soon answered.

A merflid arises from the sea. The thing is ghastly. It sports the head of a gilled wild bore. Green flesh bristles with porcupine-like needles and reeks of fish and death. It regards you with coal black eyes. You want to dry heave.

Salvatore/Timmy grins from ear to ear. "So, are ye ready to take yer first dance with a merflid?"

You recoil. "God no!"

"It'll be yer loss."

"I'm not going to have sex with that . . . that *thing*!"

Salvatore/Timmy laughs. "I didn't tell ye to have sex. I told ye to *dance*."

"But—"

"There's nothing in the world quite like the experience."

"But—"

"Dance with the merflid, me boy."

You don't have time to say anything else. Salvatore/Timmy pushes your back. You tumble from the deck. Salvatore/Timmy calls after you as you fall:

"Ye'll thank me later!"

You slash headlong into the sea of lard.

The merflid swims towards you.

If you strangle the thing, turn to page 147.
To dance with the merflid, turn to page 66.

A row of mutant-like creatures stand in a line outside of the Captain's office, under the ceiling of eyeballs.

The White Rabbit introduces you. "We now have our Cabin Boy, the thirteenth member of our crew."

She scrapes your neck and takes you down the line, starting at the end, to the lowest level crew members. "You have met Eggy Joe and Studio." She says of the leaky pirate and the wheeler. Then she introduces you to the others.

Frog Girl: a dirty teenaged girl with green freckles and slimy hair.

Tendon: a tall bony man with long white hair. Either elderly or very young.

Trapface: the cleanest member of the crew, almost polished clean. She wears a fishnet bikini that barely covers her cartoonishly large breasts, and instead of a head she has some kind of hollow steel helmet with an open bear trap for a face.

Lox: a man evolved from a walrus. Not much different than a walrus other than his humanlike arms and legs. For clothing, he wears leather bondage straps across his chest, a choke collar, and a leather g-string.

Pussy Rot: a large woman with distorted leprosy features. An eye sinking to one side of her face. A hand with bulgy grown-together fingers. She appears to be the ship's cook and her facial expression indicates that she would love to chop you up and eat you.

Eve, Said, Kumi, and Saryn: the White Rabbit's four lieu-tenants. They are demonic faeries with black butterfly wings and red hair twisted into wild spikes and screws. Their clothes have been mostly ripped away into small strips of fabric, revealing chainmail pant-

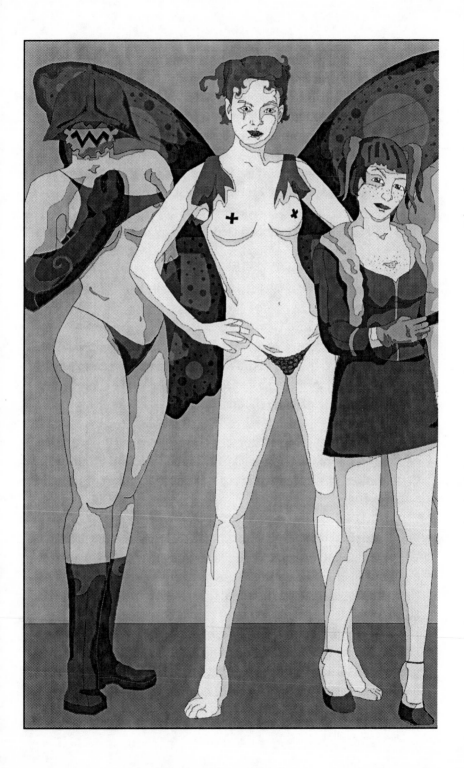

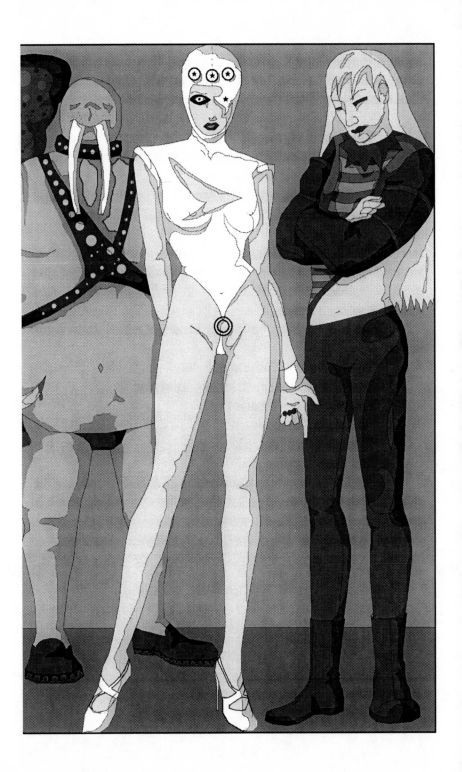

ies and electrical tape Xs over their nipples. They look a little Japanese and a little Russian, but their eyes are white and behind their blood-red lips are fangs like a vampire's, or maybe a snake's.

"Now get ready to sail," White Rabbit says to the crew.

The mutants make buzzing noises and fade into the background.

She turns to you, licking the sweat from your neck. "Let's get you plugged in. I can feel this ship aching for her cabin boy."

The Captain making squeak-rip noises in her plastic outfit as she leads you down a spiral staircase to a small room made of blue glass. It is mostly empty but for a small cabinet in a corner. And inside the cabinet: a metal box.

She lifts the box above your head and raises an eyebrow tattoo.

"Now put this on," she says to you.

An electric current pulses through the box.

You step back. "What is that?"

"The cabin," she says.

"What is it for?" you ask.

"It is for doing your job."

On closer inspection, it looks to be a miniature version of the ship. It even has the mold and sludge, wires and spikes. But it is some kind of helmet. And it seems to be leaking liquid electricity, rivers of lightning that drip down White Rabbit's arms and chest.

If you put on the helmet, turn to page 41.
If you refuse to put on the helmet, turn to page 71.

You decide to board The Eye World, stepping closer to the great metal beast, looking for an entrance . . .

The electric pulsing becomes throbbing as you reach the end of the pier. There doesn't seem to be any way to get into the ship. It oozes a sludgy pepper-toad stench that makes your eyes water.

Buried under some fuzzy black mold, you see a chain link ladder. It stretches up the side of the ship many stories above you. But it doesn't seem to go anywhere. It ends halfway to the roof.

If you take the ladder turn to page 76
If you want to call out for help turn to page 105.

The Rotten Sore seems the best bet. It's not nearly as freaky as *The Eye World*. Besides, you liked punk rock when you were a teenager. It gave you an outlet when everyone was taunting you in school, pulling your pants down and laughing at your underwear.

You walk towards the ship. A thin rope leads up to the deck. It doesn't look very secure, but you have no other option. By the time you reach the top, your hands are chaffed and bloody. You look around.

Everything seems normal, nothing cube-esque or electro-weird like the other ship. If it weren't for all the punk stuff, the vessel could pass for something straight out of a movie.

The deck is empty. You spot the captain's quarters and motion in that direction. Perhaps you'll find someone there. You take a few steps before falling flat on your face. The opening cords of *Anarchy in the UK* accompany your spill. It's an ear-shattering blast.

Your knees feel sore and your ears ring, but you're okay. No damage done. You look around and see that you've tripped over thick brass strings connected to the stern. Just a few feet from where you fell, a large hole gapes in the deck like the pit in the center of a guitar. It's as though the ship's body is a giant sounding board.

A door swings open. You turn to face the sound. A gaggle of pirates pour onto the deck. They don't look like punks at all. In fact, they look like senile old men. They smell like senile old men, too. A pissy/shitty scent wafts on the breeze.

Soon they are close enough to touch. One waves a stained and smelly bedpan in your face. Another looks at you with cloudy eyes as he smacks his lips. A long-dead parrot rests on his shoulder. Only a skeleton remains. Some, you now realize, aren't dressed like pirates at all. A toothless, skin and bone man wears panties and a pointy pink bra. To his left, a pirate has newspapers glued to his body in strategic locations. More than a few are completely naked.

These pirates and more form a circle around you. You feel their stare.

If you run like hell, turn to page 70.
If you stay, turn to page 44.

Eggy Joe takes you into an elevator. It is surprisingly clean and perhaps even *posh* with its marble-tiled walls and turquoise buttons. Like the elevator of a luxurious hotel, from the 80's. The half-electronic man cleans his wheels before entering and holds plastic cups under Eggy Joe's elbows to make sure he doesn't drip onto the leaf-patterned carpeting.

But once it starts moving, the elevator generates a loud roaring-engine noise that makes your breath hurt. All illusions of elegance leave your mind as you grind your fingers into fists.

Eggy Joe has his eyes bugged at you as you ride up.

"We'll finally be able to go back to sea," he screams over the elevator roar, poking his bony finger under your rib, "now that we have our cabin boy."

You get off on the twenty-fourth floor, the top floor, and step into a world of eyes. In the walls, in the ceiling, on pillars and even some parts of the floor there are living human-like eyes of all sizes and colors. Most of them turning to your direction. Staring. Blinking. One the size of a cow ogles out of the ceiling above you. Goo-smack noises when it blinks.

Eggy Joe walks you through the eyeball-collaged deck and into a small office. It is dark and empty, lit by a few dangling light bulbs. Just a desk covered in hundreds of blank pieces of paper. Tiny eyes in the corners.

"Here we are," the leaky pirate says.

He knocks on a metal locker in a corner.

"Captain, your new cabin boy has arrived," he says to the locker.

He knocks again on the locker and then opens the door.

Inside, there is only a baseball bat and a lot of stickiness.

"Captain, come look at him, you're going to like him," he says to the baseball bat.

"Are you playing another retard game?" asks a voice that echoes through metal.

"No, Captain." Eggy Joe smiles wicked teeth at you. "He's

really here this time. And he's already got the crooked nose that you like. You won't have to break it."

You hear rattling metal and then a head peeks down through the inside ceiling of the locker. A bald woman's head wearing black goggles that zoom in and out at you.

"He *iiiisssss* here," says the Captain. "Beautiful."

She slides down out of the locker and leaps at you with a huge smile. A tall woman. Barefoot and still almost a foot taller than you. She is completely naked other than the goggles and some machine grease. Her body is completely hairless, but she has tattoos of eyebrows where her eyebrows should be. And there are metal thorns growing from her arms and legs like a rose bush.

"Yes, yes," says the Captain, her voice teeming with childlike animation.

She grips your chin with her right hand—an almost cybernetic hand, with wires and claws woven into her pale gray flesh. Sharp points on her finger tips stab into your neck as deep as they can without breaking the skin.

Examining all sides of your face for a while. Every minute detail of your skin, especially your nose. And your eyes remain at the same level as her lips, which are a dark gray color. At first you think it is lipstick, but you are close enough to see the color is natural. And her nipples, pointing at your neck, are the same smoky color.

"You might be perfect," she says and steps away from you, behind her desk.

She removes the goggles from her face to reveal a hole instead of a left eye. It fizzles with electric sparks. You try to look away, but the popping of electricity coming from inside of her head has you in a trance. She straightens her back, loses the smile. And covers the eyehole with a white vinyl eyepatch.

"Cabin Boy is a big responsibility on this ship," the Captain says, her voice now firm and antqueen-like. "Only the strongest and wisest can handle the job."

She pulls on a white vinyl catsuit to match her eyepatch. It is sleeveless and hooded, and forms tight to her body. So much that she

still appears to be naked, but now has shiny white plastic skin. And just above her ass is a fluffy bunny tail.

"I am your Captain, your Queen, your Master," says the woman. "My name is Static Flex, but I'm more widely known as The White Rabbit."

She doesn't have any bunny ears though. Too tough for bunny ears. She looks dressed up to arouse someone with a scuba fetish.

"I expect you to follow my orders without question or hesitation," says the white queen. "Otherwise you will be treated as a mutineer and be raped to death on the spot by either myself or one of my crew."

She snaps a razor nail at Eggy Joe. "Get the others."

Then her one working eye sinks deep into you.

"Time to meet the rest of the crew."

Turn to page 17.

You run towards the mess hall, towards Piratebeard. It's the last thing you thought you'd ever do.

But Piratebeard is no longer there. The other pirates remain, sitting on benches or laying out— either face up or face down —on the floor.

You wonder where he might have gone. He had seemed so eager to see you use the dildo on the squid.

Against your better judgment, you approach a pirate. He's busy looking at his left shoe and laughing, so you punch his shoulder. It takes eight punches, but the man finally looks up. White, nearly pupil-less eyes regard you.

"Hey, it's the kissyman!" He tugs at the shirt of the pirate closest to him. "Look! Look! It's the kissyman!"

"Yes, yes," you say, talking so quickly that your words slur together. "It's the kissyman. But can you tell me where Piratebeard went?"

"Oh yes, kissyman. Anything for ye."

The pirate falls silent.

You tap your feet. "Come on, tell me!"

The man looks confused. "Tell ye what?"

"Where Piratebeard went!"

"Who's Piratebeard?"

You want to claw your eyes out. You want to scream. But another pirate turns from eating a skittering cockroach he'd found on the floor.

"He had to run to the bilge," he says. "Told us to tell ye to stay put, he did. Said he was getting something special for ye to dance with."

"Where's the bilge!"

The pirate smiles. Then he ogles your package.

"I said *where is the bilge!*"

The pirate turns his thumb downwards while still ogling your package. His answer will have to suffice.

Turn to page 101.

Captain Piratebeard brings you to the mess hall. It's a filthy, stagnant place filled with lines of overturned tables and unvarnished benches. Wooden plates and bowls caked with rotten food sit atop the few upright tables.

Piratebeard stops in the center of the room. He bends down and picks up a discarded scrubbing brush. With a smile, he hands it to you.

"Scrub the floor, matey. Yes, yes – get that dirt and grime for Merdelan. Wash the filth away. And hiker yer netherside up a bit more, too. Good, good."

Those in attendance leer and make provocative gestures with fingers and tongues.

"Now do a pirate dance!"

"But I don't know any pirate dances."

Piratebeard waves you off. "Just make it up as ye go along."

You don't know what to do. You don't want to dance for these hideous people. You don't want to dance for *anybody*. But you're scared and vulnerable and god knows what Piratebeard will do if you don't follow orders.

You break into what you believe might be a jig. Then you mimic a dance you saw Gene Kelly do in an old Technicolor movie. You remember he was wearing a sailor's suit and think the pirates might appreciate a reenactment.

Piratebeard interrupts you. "A little more pelvic thrusting, matey. Come on, get yer hips into it!"

You feel dirty, like worms are crawling across your skin, but you do what he says.

Piratebeard claps his hands, hooting and hollering. "Yeah! Make those jewels jangle!"

A pirate from the audience gets caught up in the moment. He reaches out and slaps your ass. *Hard*. Piratebeard gives him an angry glare; his hand drops away. But you don't have time to restart your dance. Another pirate takes the opportunity to tug at your briefs. Piratebeard doesn't take kindly to this and lops the man's hand off with his sword.

"Ya varlet! Only the captain touches the kissyman!"

You stop dancing. This is too much. You're sick of being used as some sort of homosexual pin-up fantasy toy.

You open your mouth to speak but, at that moment, a pirate bursts into the room, screaming.

"We're entering Satan's Mullet!"

"Satan's Mullet!" Piratebeard shouts. "*Satan's Mullet*! Everyone close yer eyes and close yer eyes *now*!"

"But I was lookin' at the kissyman," one protests.

"Damn ye!" the captain rages, "Do as I say! And that's a order!"

You don't know if this is real or if Piratebeard just wants your eyes closed so he can take advantage of you. The ship is, after all, still harbored.

But you've never seen the captain quite so adamant. Another pirate protests, says he's getting an eyeful of kissyman, but Piratebeard bounds from his seat and slaps the man's face.

Your eyes dart back and forth. You don't want something bad to happen if you don't close your eyes. But you don't want something bad to happen if you *do* close your eyes.

So what do you do?

If you keep your eyes open, turn to page 87.

If you close them, turn to page 60.

Your sanity makes a break for it. Too much swirling madness; too much contradiction. Your brain can't process it all so it shuts down completely.

You make monkey sounds with your mouth. Salvatore/Timmy soon loses interest and goes looking for another co-conspirator. But you don't stop once your audience disappears. You make monkey sounds for five straight years until you die of AIDS-related dysentery in a private room aboard *The Rotten Sore*.

THE END

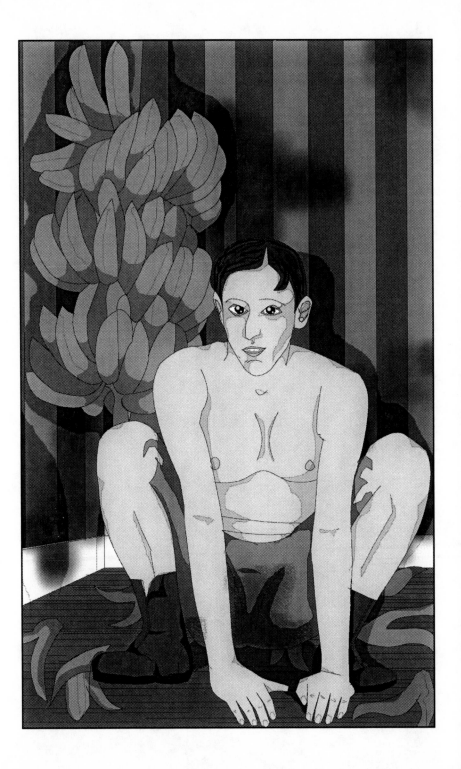

You refuse the timbers.
Piratebeard kills you.

THE END

You definitely don't want her to stop, so she takes you into the shadows and down a thin hallway. She puts a finger to her lips and tip-toes through the hall to the door on the end.

Once you are inside she whispers, "The dead are alive in those rooms."

You are in a barn, lit by several lanterns plugged into the ceiling. The floors are covered in hay. Haystacks and pitchforks in one corner. You begin to wonder why there's a barn on a pirate ship, but it makes your erection sag to think about this. So you concentrate on Frog Girl's smooth glowing butt.

She takes you up a ladder and onto a loft.

"Nobody will find us up here," she says, laying you into a bed of hay.

Her tongue moves slow against your body. She licks your thighs and asshole. You ache to fuck her, but she just smiles and pushes your hands away when you go for her vagina. She loves teasing you.

Pinning your hands behind your neck, she stretches her tongue down to her crotch and gives herself oral sex, warming herself up for you.

Just as she lowers herself into your lap, your penis touching her deep green forest, red lights begin flashing around you. A loud honking sound whales out of the ceiling.

"Shit!" Frog Girl screams, leaping away from you.

"What?" you ask.

"The alarm," she slides down the ladder, head jerking in every direction. "The Eye World is sinking. We have to abandon ship."

"Abandon ship?" you climb down the ladder after her.

"It's all my fault," she says. "I wasn't at my post."

The ship is tilting forward. The floor becomes an angle and you slip from your feet.

"Fuck fuck fuck," Frog Girl says. "We're so fucked!"

She runs around the room, able to keep her balance on the angled floor. Bending metal sounds all around you as if the cube is getting ready to implode.

"We'll never get to the life boats in time," she says.

Then she lunges at a pitchfork and begins moving stacks of hay out of the corner.

"Help me," she screams.

So you help move stacks of hay as the angle of the floor increases. Lack of balance keeps you on your knees.

A manhole is uncovered after the last stack of hay and Frog Girl opens it with her pitchfork.

"It's the only way out," she says.

You look into the hole. It is thick with sewage.

You race to get out of the ship, completely naked. Frog Girl far ahead of you, hopping with powerful legs. Through a sludgy rancid sewer tunnel.

It opens into a large room full of slime and chucks of scrap metal. The exit is in view: a jagged hole in the side of the ship.

Frog Girl squeals as her ankle gets caught in razor wire. She thrashes her leg, but it just digs deeper into her skin. Some kind of rotten mermaid creature emerges from the muck, also entangled in the wire, and grabs the girl/frog around the waist, rubbing against her with muddy tits and fishy hair.

"Keep going," Frog Girl tells you. "I'll be there in a minute."

You nod and move on. But the ship is at such an angle that you can't keep on your feet anymore. You practically have to climb up the floor to get to the hole.

Before you know what's happening, you are out in the ocean. Up to your waist in thick globs of animal fat. The ship is gone. Already under the floppy waves. You are all alone. Nothing but miles and miles of salty lard. You soon realize that it is quite impossible to swim in it. You can float by keeping still. But moving your limbs causes the ooze to suck you under.

So you're slowly sinking, not moving a muscle. You are coated in a stench like moldy bacon, and rising and falling with the waves.

Luckily, the waves are small. Any bigger and they would bury you inside of the flab.

You see a winged creature flying above you. It looks like one of the Captain's lieutenants. One of the demon faerie women. You consider signaling to her, but you fear moving your arms will pull you under. Perhaps you should just call to her. But will she be able to hear you over the loud bubbling smacking noises?

If you want to wave your arms to get the lieutenant's attention, turn to page 92.

If you call out to the lieutenant without waving your arms, turn to page 168.

The Eye World petrifies you. *The Rotten Sore* looks rough and tumble. You doubt anything positive will happen if you board either ship.

You turn away.

But the town—it doesn't feel safe, either. You've never seen so many weird people crammed into one place. But at least you won't have to learn about ships or navigation. Learning's something you hate.

From the beach you cross over onto another dusty road. Again, tattered shacks line both sides. Drunken pirates slump on porches or lie face down in the street. You step over these people and try not to make eye contact with the rest.

Inanimate objects become your chief focus. A sign on what you assume is a restaurant says GRUEL. THE HOLE might be a hotel or a brothel. Either way, it looks like a sty.

You don't want to enter any of these places—but you want desperately to sit down and rest. Soon, a sign hanging from a slightly more composed shack catches your eye:

You walk up to the business. The door stands ajar so you step in.

An antique register sits atop an unfinished wooded slab. The pirate/cashier seems either unconscious or dead. You step quietly past him.

Floorboards groan beneath your feet. The ceiling sags. At one point, moldy plaster scrapes against your head.

You've seen abandoned outhouses in better shape.

But then you notice a display tucked in the rear of the shop.

Lines of neatly stacked merchandise fill three polished, intricately carved shelves. You walk up to them, marveling at tiny little pirate ships encased in glass bottles.

Further down sits a tray of plastic medallions stamped to look like doubloons. You run your fingers through them before catching sight of a Black Bart action figure. Its legs are bendable and fun.

On the bottom shelf, however, you find the ultimate prize: a selection of jockstraps, their crotches printed with different pirate heads.

You pick up a bottled ship and a Yellowbeard jockstrap. You can't wait to find a private place to put it on and feed your underwear fetish.

The man at the register is still asleep or dead. You pocket the merchandise, but not before snagging a Pirate Town postcard on the way out. It features a street lined with shacks. Big surprise.

The shop's rickety door closes behind you. You look up and gasp. Dozens of gnarly pirates stand outside the store, waiting. You feel the heat of their stare.

"I—I was just buying some stuff . . . I swear I paid for it . . . I swear—"

The man in front spits out something black and foul. He wipes his lips clean with a huge blackened hand. "I be Scurvy Tom, head of the Pirate Town Welcoming Committee."

"The Pirate Town *what*?"

He tips his hat. "We don't get many visitors around these parts, so we like to make 'em feel at home."

You walk over to the strange man, breathing out your mouth to avoid his smell. "So—you're not going to kill me?"

"Kill ye, me boy!" The pirates share a hearty laugh.

"And your friends—they're not going to kill me? Right?"

The man pats your back hard. "Right as rain. We're just going to rustle up some whores and play canasta over at *Dirty Jack's*. Care to tag along?"

You join the men as they make their way down the street. The feeling is surreal but strangely comforting. As you walk, the pirates address you one at a time.

"Come over to me place for grokfish and gruel."

"I got a little room on me floor if ye need to rest yer bones."

"Care to hear a sea chanty?"

The kind words go on and on. Your heart swells. You've never experienced such warmth from others. Open and friendly, pirates are cooler than anyone you knew back in Wyoming. They live in shacks, yes. They stink, yes. But those things seem minor, insignificant, even.

Perhaps you'll stay in Pirate Town longer than you imagined.

And the years pass . . .

At age 29, you change your name to Black Roger.

At age 32, you replace your left leg with a slick, oaken peg. The procedure hurts – the surgeon uses no anesthesia—but, in the end, it's worth both the pain and the doubloons spent.

At age 34, you gouge out your left eye. The patch you wear is now functional as well as cosmetic.

At age 37, you shack up with Scabby Joe—a gruff yet surprisingly tender pirate who understands your needs.

At age 40, your molesting days are far behind you. With Scabby Joe, you adopt feral, three-headed children. No longer will they eat rodents in the festering back alleys of Pirate Town. A happy, shack-like home awaits them.

At age 42, you become mayor of Pirate Town. The city prospers under your reform-minded tenure. *Fortune 500* companies line six-lane streets. Celebrities build vacation homes by lardy shores.

At age 45, you leave office and pursue a career in film.

At age 53, you return to Pirate Town after winning the first ever Academy Award for porn. Six days later, you choke on a grokfish steak and die, having never once stepped foot in the sea of lard

THE END

You don't want to touch the thing. You don't want it anywhere near you. But Piratebeard is more unpredictable than you initially thought. Perhaps it's in your best interest to humor him. Grimacing, you force yourself to speak:

"Okay, I'll take the damn thing."

"That's the spirit, me boy!" Piratebeard drops the turd into your hand. "Cherish it for all times!"

"I will." You pocket the treasure. The smile on your face almost crumbles. "Count on it."

The captain pats your pocket, squashing the turd against your clothes. "But there's so much more where that came from. Ye should see the room where we store our treasure. By Merdelan, it's brimming!"

You don't want to think about this, so you don't.

"Ah! But I must tell ye about—"

The captain is interrupted by the sound of his bedchamber's door smashing open. An ancient pirate bounds in. His eyes are wide; his arms flail above his head.

"Captain Piratebeard! Captain Piratebeard! I've found treasure!"

The captain turns to him. "And where did ye find it?"

"'Twas in the chamber pot in me room!"

"Good, good. Now hand it over."

The pirate obeys. Piratebeard taps the treasure with his fingers, gauging its firmness. While you find this disgusting, horror doesn't overtake you until the captain lifts the turd to his mouth. He stares down at it, enraptured, before biting the end like a prospector testing gold.

"It be pure, me boy!" He beams. "Good work!"

The man curtsies.

"Carry it to the storeroom. Take inventory, too."

"Yes, Captain! *Seig Heil!*"

Piratebeard responds with a peace sign before dismissing the man. He turns in your direction.

You haven't moved since watching Piratebeard bite the turd. You want to talk, but your mouth simply hangs there.

"Now where were we? Ah yes, I was about to tell ye about the upcoming festivities."

"But—"

Tomorrow be my birthday—a *very special* birthday at that. Attendance is mandatory."

"But—"

"It'll be a grand celebration."

You finally spill it out. "But you just bit that . . . *thing*!"

"Aye. That I did."

Your hands quake. Captain Piratebeard is right; it's time to go to bed. Time to lose yourself in sleep and forget everything. "Could you just show me where I'm going to stay. I'm really tired."

"Of course, me boy. The first day is always the roughest, and ye must be rested for the party!"

Turn to page 133.

You feel the needle first, as the White Rabbit lowers the cabin onto your head. It feels as thick as a pencil when it breaks through your skull and slides easily into your delicate brain matter. She tightens straps around your forehead and under your chin. It is absurdly heavy, too much for your neck muscles so you have to hold it up with both hands.

You look at the Captain with a wrinkled face, about to complain, when fluids begin filling the inside of your mind. Your flesh is becoming loose and melting off of your body. Fuzzy-brained.

White Rabbit explains the sensations to you as you feel them: Your body and mind is infusing itself with the ship. First, you will feel like the cabin on your head is becoming an extension of your body. You will feel just the exterior of the cabin at first, but soon your nerves will join with the insides. It is a miniature replica of The Eye World, and you can feel every level, every room, every piece of furniture inside of the cube. The replica is exact in every detail. Now you should be feeling the connection between the miniature replica and The Eye World. You will feel like you are in two places at the same time. At first, you probably won't be able to distinguish the real ship from the box on your head. And your body from the forehead down should soon feel as if it is underneath the ocean of lard. You might feel as if you are drowning, but don't panic. It is only a trick of the senses. Lastly, you will be able to see out of the eyes inside of The Eye World. It will be overwhelming at first. You will be practically blinded by all of all the visions crowding your mind. Concentrate on one eye at a time. Close your real eyes. The ship's eyes will start to focus. One of the eyes will be more clear than the others. It should jump out at you. It will probably be the one in this room. The one looking down on us. Focus on that eye and try to close all others. Look around the room with it. When you are comfortable and feel in control, try opening a second eye. You will eventually be able to see through every eye in the ship.

White Rabbit leaves you to get acquainted with your new found body extension. It is very chaotic. You can see everything that is happening on the ship. You can see Eggy Joe and Studio mopping the ceiling, Pussy Rot licking curly wigs in the kitchen, Lox eating gumbo on an old treasure chest. Not only can you see them, but you can feel them inside of the ship. It feels like they are inside of you. Moving around inside of your head.

The Captain is outside kissing one of her demon faerie girls. Licking her ear and neck. You can feel the faerie girl writhe inside of you like she is getting oral sex, rubbing against what feels to be your brain. This gives you an erection, but you try to ignore it. You close that ship's eye and try to concentrate on someone else: Frog Girl. But she is getting ready to fuck the mantis-like man, Tendon.

"Do they ever give it a rest?" you ask yourself, as other members of the crew take a break from their duties to sexually indulge themselves.

White Rabbit hyper-snickers when she sees your cock in your hand.

"The Cabin Boy is always the horniest crew member on board," she says.

You zip up your pants and try to pretend like it was nothing.

"It's time to shove off. Come with me to the helm."

She takes you into a room with a floor that moves under your feet like a treadmill.

"You pilot the ship here," White Rabbit says. "In this room and nowhere else. You pilot the ship by moving in the direction we want the ship to be moving. Unless the anchor is down, as it is now. Never leave this room if the anchor is weighed. Traveling down a floor with the anchor raised will cause the ship to plunge into the ocean. If you need anything, Frog Girl will get it for you. You can call her by hitting any of the red buttons on the balance bars."

After a little practice, the Captain has you take the ship out. She says you can go anywhere to the south or west. It's just for practice. You have to get more accustomed to The Eye World before you'll be ready to loot merchant ships.

If you want to go south, turn to page 81.
If you want to go west, turn to page 64.

Perhaps it's best to stay, your mind reasons. Spending months at sea with nutty old pirates is better than being cooped up in a mainland jail. Besides, they like The Sex Pistols, so they can't be all bad.

Still, their stares make you uncomfortable. They remind you of your grandfather when he was senile and psychotic. You dealt with flying obscenities and fecal matter then, but he was just one person. And your grandfather was a factory worker, not a pirate.

You draw in a deep breath to compose yourself. Only then do you speak:

"Uh, I'm here to apply for the navigator position."

"Speak up!" a naked pirate shouts. "We can't hear ye!"

You repeat yourself, this time louder.

"We still can't hear ye! Got a grokfish in yer mouth, boy?"

Again, you repeat yourself.

The pirates still don't understand. One by one, they lose interest. Some turn their gazes skyward. Others fiddle with their clothes. A few flail their bodies in mimicry of dancing. You wave your arms and shout, but no one acknowledges you.

You sink to the floorboards. You wrap your hands around your face. The voyage will be miserable if you have to spend it with people like this. Would they remember to feed you? Did they even think to bring food?

At that moment a slightly younger man emerges from the captain's chamber. He walks with a steady, purposeful gait. His eyes seem clear and alert, not rheumy or dead. He wears simple clothes: a billowy white shirt and a pair of brown trousers. The man walks in another direction, but notices you and changes his path. He reaches where you sit and extends his hand.

"Salvatore's the name, but ye can call me Timmy. I be the cabin boy on this vessel."

You return his greeting. At least someone on the ship isn't senile.

"So what brings ye to *The Rotten Sore*? Don't reckon I've seen ye here before."

"I was hoping to talk to the captain," you reply.

"Really?" He eyes you suspiciously. "And what business have ye with Captain Rotgut?"

You bite your lip, afraid to say the wrong thing. Hands clench nervously. Eyes wander over to the plank. "I need to get away and become a pirate. I mean no harm."

"Want yer sea legs do ye?" Salvatore/Timmy pats your back. "Well, that be an admirable goal!"

"But I don't know about your. . . shipmates. Maybe this isn't the place for me."

"Don't worry, me lad. Ye'll get used to 'em."

You nod. The man seems level headed so you assume he knows what he's doing. Maybe things will go smoothly with him on board. Maybe he'll contain the senile old goats.

"But come, I'll take ye to Captain Rotgut. He'll talk to ye. See if ye be seaworthy."

You nod and follow close behind.

Turn to page 72.

You get a blue-striped bowl filled with beans and white chunks of fat that you assume is the pork part. But it is food so you are happy. You sit down at a table and block all senses except taste, closing all of the ship's eyes as well as your regular eyes.

Before you can finish, you hear a woman's voice over the intercom.

"Zhotrax ships approaching," she says in a calm voice. "We are under attack."

And an emergency siren comes on, accompanied by flashing lights.

The two vampire faeries grab you from behind.

"No time to go to the helm," one of them says.

"You must pilot the ship from here," the other says.

They raise the anchor for you and push you away from them, telling you to run as fast as you can.

White Rabbit bursts into the room from the stairwell, screaming profanities at you. She pulls out an electric whip and lashes at you to make you move faster. You run until you are against the wall and can't go any farther.

"Run in place!" White Rabbit screams, whipping you repeatedly.

You try to move your legs as fast as you can, but the whipping is slowing you down. Every time she hits you your legs become weak and want to collapse. Then the whip catches your left foot and you tumble to the ground, head-first.

The ship falls with you. Plunging into the ocean of lard. And when the cabin smashes into the floor, you feel the hull of the ship break open. Your body goes into shock. As if it was your skull that has been broken open instead of the box on your head.

The Captain continues he screaming assault. She kicks you in the stomach and then in the face. Your mind is draining and you can't feel pain anymore. The captain doesn't try to get you up, she just wants to cause serious damage. You see her heel stabbing into your head. It breaks one of your eyes open. She kicks the cabin as well, shoving her heels through its metal casing which causes holes to suddenly open up in the ship. Eggy Joe is crushed under one of her heels while trying to escape via lifeboat.

As you drift away from consciousness, away from your body, your eyes closing, you look down at yourself through the ship's eyes. You see yourself being beaten into a bloody mess. Most of the crew surrounding you. Taking turns beating you as the room slowly fills with lard from the sea. Until the Captain stabs a large iron pipe through the cabin on your head, which plunges through the real ship and crushes you through the floor.

THE END

The opening chords of *Anarchy in the UK* jerk you out of sleep. You awaken to a herd of stampeding pirates. You turn over quickly, just in time to avoid their feet. Why is everyone in such a hurry? Then you remember it's the captain's birthday.

You follow the influx. Sunrays sting your eyes. You notice the ship still hasn't set sail, though *The Eye World* is gone.

The pirates file into a room adjacent to the captain's quarters. All except for one, that is. A comatose pirate rolls with the ship in his wheelchair. You wonder if he had been left out all night, but aren't quite concerned enough to help.

You grit your teeth. A pirate continues to bang on the strings connected to the stern. *Anarchy in the UK* gets louder and louder with every strike. You can't figure out why he's still banging away. Everyone's awake and outside.

No matter.

You pause behind the door everyone had entered. Ear to the wall, you listen.

Sounds like lots of reverie. Lots of *weird* reverie. Someone bellows. Hundreds respond with groaning, flapping, or sloshing sounds. You brace yourself. Minutes pass. Then you push the door open.

Captain Piratebeard sits enthroned on a golden, filigreed chair. It rests atop a rotating pedestal elevated at least twenty feet in the air. A massive floor-to-ceiling navigation wheel spins behind him. It appears to be *papier mache,* like a huge stage prop.

Ancient pirates writhe on the floor beneath this tableau, one piled atop the other. The mass looks like a writhing, organic ball. Gnarled hands reach up to stroke the pedestal before being beaten away by other hands wanting to do the same. Salvatore/Timmy doesn't appear to be amongst the lot. You find this odd. He had sounded so excited about the party.

You turn to the pedestal as Piratebeard unleashes a shriek.

"*I am yer salvation!*" His fists slam the bejeweled armrest. "*Yer salvation! Yer salvation!*"

The other pirates wring their hands and rend their clothes at the sound of his voice.

"When all others fail, I shall be yer deliverance!"

A few worshipers foam at the mouth. Others develop stigmata – but you can see they're really smashing ketchup packets or tiny rodents against their palms.

"I am omnipotent!" Piratebeard raises a tin crown from his lap and places it atop his head. "I see all! I know all! I *feel* all! The secrets of the universe belong to me! I alone sit at Merdelan's side!"

You watch the proceedings in continued awe. Finally, Piratebeard pulls a switch. The pedestal descends on hydraulics. Once the throne reaches floor-level, Piratebeard stands. He makes a strange sign with his fingers and walks towards you, arms outstretched. The other pirates remain on the floor.

"Behold majesty, me boy."

Piratebeard doesn't look any different to you.

Twig-like arms encircle your shoulders. The captain leans over and speaks just inches from your ear. His voice is slithery, serpent-like: "Seventy-four years ago, on a strange shore, an ancient gypsy spoke of destiny. On my hundredth birthday, said she, I was to take my place amongst the gods and goddesses of pirate lore."

Maritime music swirls. From where it comes, you cannot say.

"'Twas a lad of 26 then. Didn't think I'd make it to 40 on these rough and tumble seas, but destiny has a way of catching up with ye, it does. *Praise Merdelan!*"

"Praise Merdelan!" The crew shouts in unison.

Captain Piratebeard looks at his gnarled and twisted hands. He sighs. "These bones are a century old. It seems like yesterday when—"

"But ye're only 99, Captain Piratebeard," a toothless pirate interrupts. "I know 'cause—"

The captain stamps his foot down on the speaker's hand.

"But come, have ye some cakes and have ye some lard!" Piratebeard leads you to a table laden with food and drink. You were so enraptured by Piratebeard's floorshow that you didn't notice the banquet.

But one look at the spread causes you to grimace. The stuff is sticky, prickly, and/or seaweed-filled. And the centerpiece! It's the head of a repulsive wild boar/fish hybrid. An apple is wedged in its horror-jaws. Confetti and streamers drizzle down below glassy eyes.

"Eat!" The captain hands you a hideous cake. "Merdelan commands it!"

You stuff the green biscuit-thing into your mouth. It tastes like a snot and oyster pancake baked with too much salt. You force it down with a lopsided smile: "Yummmm."

Piratebeard pats your back. "I knew ye'd like it, me boy! It's a ceremonial birthday biscuit. Baked with me precious semen, it is. An ancient Babylonian recipe."

You spit on the floor, your stomach seizing in knots.

"Too rich for ye, me lad?"

You just nod.

"But it's time for the event we've all been waiting for. After all, this is more than just a birthday celebration. It's a party for *ye*, too." Piratebeard raises his arms and, in a booming, god-like voice, shouts: "*Shiver me timbers!*"

You recoil then scream. Horrible flapping tendrils, like those of a jellyfish only larger, extend from slits in both his shirt and jacket.

They pulse, glowing red then blue then yellow.

"Oh my god! What are those things?"

"Why they're timbers, me boy. All pirates worth their salt have 'em." Piratebeard's eyes gleam. "And, today, ye'll get yer timbers, too."

You pull away. "No! No, I don't want them! Stay back!"

"And I'm honored that ye could receive them on this most special of days."

"Please, please! I'll do anything you ask!"

Captain Piratebeard advances as lights dim, and pirates pick themselves up from off the floor and don satanic black and red robes.

If you refuse the timbers, turn to page 32.

If you accept, turn to page 103.

You are on a small island. Actually, it is more like a bunch of rocks sticking out of the water. There aren't any trees or plants or bugs. Just rocks and the two of you.

You learn that the woman who rescued you was not the same one you saw in the air before you were attacked by the whale/turtle creature. That means one of her sisters is still alive. She says it must be her oldest sister, Eve. She knows this because she accidentally left her other two sisters, Said and Saryn, handcuffed to each other in their bedroom.

Waking from a nap, you find the faerie woman in a lifeboat that washed onto shore, eating the people on board. You come for a closer look. It is Eggy Joe and his wheeler friend, Studio. She is coated in blood, ripping into them with her fangs and sucking the juice from them.

When she sees you, she looks up from a severed arm in her hands.

"Sleep well?" she asks and drinks from the limb.

You nod.

You're not sure whether she killed the men or if they were dead before the boat landed. Her eyes are cold at you. Whipping her dreadlocks into the air when she tears into the meat.

At night, she wraps you around her and sucks on your shoulder like a nipple. She says she wants to fuck you in the morning, and then go look for her sister. You're sure she's just keeping you around for food. Wondering if she is like a black widow spider and plans to bite into you just as she has an orgasm in the morning.

She sleeps. Tickling your hips with her wings, drooling against your neck, and her lips stretched tight into a smile.

You feel like a teddy bear under her muscled arms as you drift off into sleep.

THE END

As the Captain's personal slave, you are forced to do any task that she commands. And one task is to become the ship's whore. Your body is to be used as a fucking machine any time a crew member requires your services. And by the looks of things, that should be every other hour for the rest of your life.

Frog Girl takes you down to the torture dungeon and removes your clothes.

"Here are the new ones," she says with a froggy smile, handing you a dog's choke collar and a leather thong.

"Don't worry," she says to you, wrapping her arm around your neck like a childhood pal. "It won't be too bad. Everybody's really good at sex here. You'll have lots of fun."

Like the crack of a whip, she snatches a beetle on the floor with her frog tongue and opens her lips to show you its writhing legs before gulping it down.

"I'll show you," she says, sliding her pirate clothes off and taking you by the hand into a dark corner.

Her flesh is pale with a lime-tint, covered in green freckles and scars. Her shiny eyes face you as she rubs her smooth webbed fingers against your cock until it grows hard. She kisses down your chest with girlish giggles.

In a snap, her frog tongue darts out and catches your cock like a fly, slurping it into her mouth. Inside of her, she is all goop and slippery meat. Like a frog's mouth. There aren't any teeth.

The girl sucks on you, eyes closed, webbed fingers against your ass force you closer to her. Even though she is hardly human, you find it incredibly pleasurable. Better than any sex you have ever dreamed about.

There is a knock at the door.

A voice: "Froggy, you're needed at the helm."

You are close to orgasm, but the girl spits you out.

Looking up at you, licking her lips and neck. "Should I go up there?" she asks. "Or should we hide in the shadows and continue?"

She winks at you and giggles like a school girl.

If you continue to have sex, turn to page 33.
If you decide she better go to the helm, turn to page 12.

You shake your head. "Sorry, but I've had a long day. All I want to do is sleep."

Salvatore/Timmy looks disappointed.

"Maybe some other time. Tomorrow, even."

He nods. "Never let it be said that I force the hands of others."

The look on the man's face is almost heartbreaking. Maybe you should have gone, but you can barely keep your eyes open as it is. You decide to offer some consolation: "I do appreciate the offer, though."

"But I'm not going to leave just yet." Salvatore/Timmy bends to the floor. "Not until I see ye back in bed."

You gulp.

"Come on, me boy. Let me help."

You don't want his aid. You want to stay on the floor, away from bugs and pickle/monkey things. But he can't know this. You're supposed to be a pirate, and pirates aren't afraid of bugs or pickle/monkey things.

Salvatore/Timmy's hands reach beneath your armpits and pull you up. You look towards the bed. The room is much darker than it had been when you went to sleep. Hundreds of red and blue eyes now flash at you. They swarm all throughout the nest of dried worms, moving fast.

Drawing in a deep breath, you lay yourself down on the worm mat. Not a second passes before the first set of prickly legs brushes against you.

"Comfortable?"

Something hellish crawls across your mouth. "Oh yes, very."

"Then I'll be going now. Will see ye at Captain Dogvomit's party."

"I'll see you there, too." Your hair is alive with insects. "Count on it."

"An interesting affair it will be."

Your skin crawls. Something pinches your leg. Something else crawls up your pants and nibbles at your scrotum.

"Much food and much lard."

You wish to god that Salvatore/Timmy would stop babbling.

"And I'd like to talk with ye personally. If—"

"Oh God, just—*please!*" The thimble-sized monkey/pickle thing plays with your ear lobe. Gently at first. Then it begins to tug.

"I'm really tired! Really tired and I want to go to sleep!"

Salvatore/Timmy bows. "I understand. Sorry to talk yer ear off at this ungodly hour."

The man sounds hurt again, but this time you don't care. You just want him gone so you can leave this godforsaken bed.

He bows yet again. You want to push him out the door. Before you can act, Salvatore/Timmy steps outside. You wait until the door closes completely. Then you jump down.

One of the bugs clings to your shirt. You tear the strange, spiral-shaped thing off and smash it against the floor. The thing is unharmed. You smash again, finally crushing the bug. You gag at the orange, goopy mess that covers your fist. A thick coppery smell hangs in the air. It makes you wince.

But the thing doesn't stay smashed. With a series of clicks and pops, the carapace reforms. Spewed guts slide back into the body cavity. You decide to let the thing be.

It soon skitters off.

Your nerves rattle, but fatigue overrides concern. You close your eyes and again fall asleep to the vibrations of a strange machine.

Turn to page 50.

You close your eyes. Perhaps an unwanted hand will try to touch you, but you've seen too many freaky things over the last day. You're not in the mood to see more if Satan's Mullet is as bad as it sounds.

You feel swimmy. Your stomach rumbles. It seems as though time and space is stretching, and that you're stretching with it. The air feels charged, static-filled.

And no one molests you. Perhaps you've made the right decision.

Ten or more minutes pass before the odd stretchy-swimmy sensations ebb. When they do, you open your eyes. You see other pirates doing the same.

"Whew!" one says. "That was close!"

Piratebeard looks up at you. "Closed yer eyes, I see. Be glad ye did, me boy. The last person who opened his eyes as he passed through Satan's Mullet . . . well . . . the less said the better."

You nod.

"But keep dancing! Satan's Mullet is behind us, so let's usher in the new age with yer sweet, sweet gyrations!"

The pirates yell and scream, but you stand there, silent and motionless.

"Flare yer timbers!" someone finally shouts.

You do so. The feeling is amazingly surreal.

"And use this, too," Piratebeard holds out a large black squid. "Make merry with it, me boy!"

You take the squid and rub it all over your body. Black ink spills across your chest. You grit your teeth in anger—but the display seems to turn Piratebeard on.

"Suck its tentacles!"

You suck its tentacles.

"Stuff its head in yer bloomers! Merdelan commands it!"

You stuff its head in your underwear. The pouch bulges obscenely.

"And give it a shake!"

You give it a shake.

"Now take this!" Piratebeard holds out a twenty-inch black dildo. "Use it on the squid!"

From outside a window, you see Salvatore/Timmy walking across the deck.

Perhaps he can help you out of this predicament.

You turn to Piratebeard. He still holds the dildo. "Uh. Hold on for a second. I . . . uh . . . have an . . . uh . . . *even bigger one* in my sleeping quarters . . . yes. Let me get it."

Piratebeard's eyes light up. "Then make haste, me boy! Make haste or may the trumpets of a thousand angels blast fire up yer ass!"

You drop the squid. You take off running.

Turn to page 162.

"*What?*"

Piratebeard closes the book. "Decapitation is what the handbook recommends, so that's what will be done. But don't worry," he soothes. "It won't be as bad as ye think."

"Not as bad as I think! How the hell could—"

The captain draws a massive sword. It's at least six-feet long and a foot thick. The edges are serrated. Piratebeard runs his fingers up and down the blade. "This'll saw through pretty quick, I tell ye."

You turn and run. The captain sprints behind you. He's fast for an old coot and catches up with you outside his office door. Piratebeard pushes your shoulder. You careen sideways. The door spills open, and you fall onto marbled office floors.

Piratebeard picks you up, dropping your body across his desk. The secretary doesn't seem to care. She just takes down the minutes of your impromptu session with the captain.

The "In" box digs hard into your back. The fax's tray smooshes your face. You can now see what the machine churns out: either blank pages or anatomically correct drawings of stick figures. But you don't have much time to survey things as Piratebeard brings the blade to your neck.

"No, Captain! Please!" You piss your pants. "Aren't we friends!"

"Of course we're friends, me boy. And ye remind me of my son, god rest 'em."

"But would you do this to your own flesh and blood!"

Piratebeard spends a moment in thought. "Well, he *was* on the lookout nest when he was supposed to be swabbing decks . . ."

Hope flies out the window. You raise your hand in defense, but the captain jumps upon your chest, straddling you. He feels supernaturally strong. A brief glint of steel, and the blade punctures the center of your throat. Agony is intense for a second. Then shock kicks in.

Piratebeard pauses, frowns at the mess dripping down his desk. "Damn it, boy! Ye're nothing but a bag of blood!"

You gurgle.

Piratebeard continues until your head rolls across his desk, and you gurgle no more.

Your body shuts down, but your head can still see, still think.

Quickly, Piratebeard brings your dripping head to a row of mounts. One holds a sea creature. Another holds a pineapple top. Your head goes on an empty one. Piratebeard plugs your bloody spinal column nub into an outlet in the mount and flicks a switch behind your left ear. Thick oak starts to vibrate, rattling your skull.

"I hate having to do this to ye, me boy. But I gotta do what the handbooks says. But the handbook didn't say I couldn't keep ye alive. It just said I had to cut off yer head."

You try to say something, but only a wheeze comes out.

"I had to cut yer vocal cords, so I wouldn't try talking. But I can keep ye company when I'm in the office, sing ye old pirate chantys, tell ye tales of the sea."

Your neck can turn a little. Just enough to see the sea creature's head mounted next to your own. You realize it's alive. The thing regards your served head with a knowing look. The clicking sound it makes is rueful.

"Ye'll last a good ten years on this mount. Just as long as the damn battery doesn't give." Captain Piratebeard turns to your headless body and grimaces. "But let's get rid of this nasty old thing. I'll be back forthwith."

Through a portal, you watch Piratebeard carry your limp body out the door. He falls out of view for a second before reappearing by the gunwall. With a heave and a ho, he tosses your body into the ocean for the grokfishes and merflids to eat. Piratebeard returns a few minutes later with a fiddle in his hands. He brings it to his neck and plays a very off-key rendition of *Wind Beneath My Wing*.

You fear this is the first of many times you'll be hearing this song.

THE END

You decide to go west, but have no clue which way is west. There isn't a compass of any kind so you just pick a direction and start moving. They'll probably let you know if you're going the wrong way.

After a minute of treading through thick lard, Frog Girl enters the room.

"Need anything?" she asks.

"No," you say. "I think I'm fine."

"You've been pressing the red button over and over again for the past hour," she says.

"No, I haven't," you say. "I've only been in here for maybe ten minutes."

"No, it's been hours," Frog Girl says.

You try to shake your head, but instead you spin around in a circle.

Frog Girl cocks her head at you.

You spin in another circle.

"What are you doing?" the girl asks.

You can't control yourself. For some reason, your body is compelled to twirl.

Soon you feel like a ballerina, spinning gracefully in circles.

But then you see it. Through the ship's exterior eyes you can see the lard spinning in circles with you.

"A whirlpool!" you cry.

You try to stop yourself from spinning. You try running in the other direction to break free. But your head is dizzy and your legs are sinking low to the ground.

Frog Girl tries to help you up, but your eyes are fading away.

Turn to page 96.

"I don't want to go," you tell them.

"We gut cowards you know," Pussy Rot says. She goes ahead of you.

The Captain stands impatiently on the other side.

"It's safe," they keep saying.

"I don't care," you say. "I have a bad feeling."

The pirates argue with each other. You can't really understand them from here.

"Okay, stay on that side," White Rabbit says. "It's safer that way. We don't want to lose the cabin."

You wave to them.

Then they walk away from the bridge and out of your view.

The day passes. You decide they aren't coming back.

You don't want to cross the log to look for them, so you walk along the beach. Barefooted with mangled creatures glopping through your toes. One fetus, a human one you think, is hooked onto a rubber rock, exposed to the red sun. Its flesh drying out. You approach it, poke it with a metallic twig and it makes rasp-whispery noises at you. Trying to cry out with underdeveloped lungs.

Overstuffed seagulls flop down next to you and peck at the beached fetus. They bite pieces off of it and thrash it around in their mouths. Taking turns on the face, until one of them bites the head off at the neck and flies away with it.

You row back to The Eye World and take it out to sea, not really sure where to go. It is much more peaceful now that you are alone. You have full control of the ship and plenty of food and water, probably enough to last you a few years. Perhaps you'll find a civilization out there somewhere and make a new life for yourself. Perhaps get a new crew to travel around with. Or rescue a woman on a deserted island somewhere and fall in love.

One thing's for sure: your adventure is only beginning.

THE END

You scream as the merflid wraps you in sticky tentacles. It retracts them, drawing your closer. A black-pinchered maw opens. The smell is overpowering. You almost lose consciousness.

A fleshy mouth-appendage extends outward. Circular and hollow, it starts to spin. You thrash against the tentacles, but their grip is unbreakable.

The appendage widens. It touches your lips and covers them, undulating in orgasmic waves. A long, bristly thing plays with your tongue. The taste is like getting French kissed by a carp.

The merflid dunks you beneath the waves. Lard fills your nose, floods your lungs. It brings you to its body, raking you across porcupine-esque stubble. The pain feels like the sting of a thousand bees.

And then something changes.

The needles, they are injecting you with something – something *cool*. Your vision goes black and then reforms inside a world of swaying purple trees. A silver brook coils between their trunks. Fawns along the bank lap water into their mouths. One looks up and speaks, but you don't understand German.

Your vision soars, past the trees, the brook, and the fawns. Over a green encrusted ridge you fly. Wind billows out your clothes. Finally your body stops, hovering over a verdant valley in which the very rocks sing. In amongst this valley, a host of naked midgets carry flaming swords.

This, you realize, is *Eden*.

Then the connection snaps, and you find yourself floating on the sea. You're not sure if an eternity has gone by or merely a second. It somehow feels like both.

You look around. The merflid is gone. Where it went, you cannot say.

You draw in a deep breath and luxuriate for a while, allowing lard waves to wash over you. The newly risen sun is apple-like and gorgeous. It seems as though you could reach up and take a bite out of it. Time spent with the merflid has energized you. You feel born-again. Energy ripples through your body, tingling all the way. You feel

ready for anything, ready to set sail on this sea of lard.

You look up at the ship. Someone is lowering a rope. You smile. Salvatore/Timmy has obviously been waiting the entire time. Now he's giving you a way back onboard.

You bid goodbye to the sweet waves of lard, take another look at the majestic sun, and wade over to the rope.

Turn to page 164.

You don't know what you're supposed to be doing so you decide to find some food. It has been a while since you've eaten. You study the insides of your head, looking through your ship's eyes until you find what looks like a cafeteria.

Take two flights of stairs down. A few others are eating here. Two of the demon faerie women are on the far side of the cafeteria. Next to you the long stick man, Tendon, is eating a bowl of soup and staring at a nail on the table. He looks like a spider sitting there. Not making any noise except the slurping of soup.

You move closer to the two women. They are pulling balls of squishy meat out of a barrel and biting into them. The flesh wads are alive; they pulse and squirm. Like a puffed veiny fetus without limbs or a head. The women rip the flesh bags open with their snake teeth and guzzle the blood and juices. One of them chews the meat and then spits it out. Once finished, the faeries toss them onto the floor and reach into the barrel for another one.

The girls turn their backs and block you from the barrel with their enormous black butterfly wings. You go to the counter that opens up to the kitchen where Pussy Rot is smoking a cigarette.

"I'm hungry," you tell her.

"Of course you are," she says, puss in the corners of her face like sideburns. "What do you want?"

She gives you a handwritten menu with three items to choose from.

If you'd like a bowl of pork and beans, turn to page 48.

If you'd like some salmon jerky and an orange, turn to page 120.

If you'd like a hand-shaped meatloaf stuffed with goat cheese, turn to page 112.

You run like hell, but you don't get very far. Before you reach the rope, your face starts to peel and bubble. It feels like an animal is scurrying around under there, wanting out. You collapse to your knees, howling in pain and confusion.

A pirate with a visible colostomy bag turns to you, his face a mask of horror. "Avast! Avast! Flesh-rotting scurvy's gone airborne!"

His mates pull their shirts over their noses, but you're too busy disintegrating to notice. You claw at your melting features, but that only causes more flesh to fall onto the planks. Your eyes pop and then drizzle down the raw meat of your cheeks. Something round and spongy runs down your leg and slides through your pants onto the deck. It's a testicle. Once muscles liquefy, your skin and clothes puddle around your feet.

Your bloody skeleton rattles and shakes. One by one, the bones drop. Your skull falls first, followed by your cervical vertebrae, clavicle, and scapula. Within a minute, you're just a pile of quivering bones in a goopy soup.

Once you've stopped moving, the gnarly old captain leaves his quarters and surveys your remains.

"Argh!" he shouts, his words muffled by a protective facemask. "Clean up this mess before I keelhaul the lot of ya!"

THE END

You shove White Rabbit away from you, liquid lightning splashing her chest. And you're frozen and don't know if you should run or apologize.

"What is wrong with you?" the Captain says, red-faced.

You shrug.

Her eyebrow-tattoos go angry at you. She leaps at you, trying to attach the cabin to your head. But you catch it, push it away. She kicks you in the stomach and you find yourself wrestling her. Her vinyl clothes rubbing burns into your knees. Blue lightning spattering in your face. Trying to keep the device from your head.

You squirm free and get to your feet.

Red eye at you.

"Joe!" she calls.

And Eggy Joe bursts through the door. He grabs you, leaking elbow fluid down your throat. The Captain lunges helmet-first.

You see the enormous needle coming at you and jerk your head back, accidentally smashing Joe's nose which loosens his grip. Dropping to the floor just in time.

You Look up: White Rabbit hits Eggy Joe instead. The needle slams into his head. He sways, eyes going blank. White Rabbit's face goes slack as she realizes what she has done.

"Sorry, Joe," the Captain says, caressing his cheek with her non-electric hand. "You'll have to be the next cabin boy."

She kisses his shivering lips and tightens the straps under his chin.

Then he collapses, asleep, electricity pumping into his body.

"Now you'll have to take over his job," the Captain says.

Her eye coiling at you.

"...As my personal assistant." And you can tell by the tone of her voice that 'assistant' is just another term for 'slave.'

Turn to page 56.

You follow the cabin boy across the deck to the captain's quarters. He pauses by a heavy oak door and gives it three knocks. Something shuffles inside. The cabin boy knocks again.

"Who goes there?" a gritty voice bellows. You steel yourself. The captain's tone sounds just as old and ragged as that of his crew.

"Timmy!" the cabin boy exclaims. "Got someone who wants to talk to ye! Says he wants to turn pirate."

"Then bring 'em in!"

The door swings open. The cabin boy steps aside, and you find yourself wilting under the captain's gaze.

Ancient yet commanding, he is dressed in full-on pirate regalia slightly too big for his frame. The captain behaves nothing like his crew as he sits, perfectly composed, behind an expensive, corporate-looking desk. Two wire baskets sit on the right end. One is labeled: *In*. The other: *Out*. On the other side, a fax machine churns out page after page of memos.

The chamber itself is equally expensive and corporate-looking. You are amazed that such a place could be found on a pirate ship. Genuine marble tiles make up the floor. The walls are white, populated with images of famous pirates and hardcore porn. Discrete track lighting accentuates the photos. To the left of the filing cabinet, a water cooler sits beneath the wall-mounted head of a bulbous, multi-eyed sea creature. There's another mount to the left of the creature, but it lies empty. An elderly, big-titted secretary rests by a stenographer's machine. She looks bored in her pink, belly-baring sweater and blue stretch pants.

The cabin boy leads you to the front of the desk. You are wary, though the captain's lips offer a welcoming smile.

"So, what brings ye to the office of Captain Piratebeard?"

Confusion piles atop confusion. That wasn't the name the cabin boy gave you. You question the captain.

"Ah, our cabin boy remembers names like a walrus remembers to exercise. Don't be surprised if he calls ye Sally." He laughs and coughs up a lung. "'Tis best not to listen to 'em."

Salvatore/Timmy bows his head. "Many apologies, Captain

Silverpeg."

"Piratebeard's the name, matey." He shoos the cabin boy away and turns to you, beckoning with a skeletal finger. "Come, take a closer look if ye want to see how I got it."

You walk over to the captain. From a distance, his beard appears knotty and unkempt. Up close, however, you see how the strands are twisted together to create hundreds of miniature, perfectly formed pirates that flow down the length of his beard. Two larger ones serve as sideburns.

"Hey, that's pretty neat! How did you get them?"

"Can't tell ye now, me boy. Maybe later. Maybe once ye've got yer sea legs."

You beam. "So, you're going to take me on!"

"Of course. I knew it as soon as ye walked in. Had that certain something ye did." Piratebeard reaches for a goblet and frowns as he sees it empty. "Secretary!"

The secretary arises from her chair by the stenographer's machine. She walks over to a bar area and pours chunky white liquid from a pitcher into a jewel-studded goblet. A tiny umbrella is placed into the mix before she brings it to Piratebeard's desk.

"Ye're a fine wench." He downs half the fluid. "Glad I hired ye."

The secretary says nothing. She reclaims her place by the stenographer's machine. There, she watches, enraptured, as Piratebeard drinks lustily.'

The lumpiness repulses you. "What the hell are you drinking?"

"It be lard from the sea, me boy!" The captain takes a final chug. "Bequeathed by Merdelan himself!"

"*Lard from the sea?*"

"Aye, 'tis a righteous bounty!"

"But why does the sea have lard in it?" You imagine the blubber of a thousand clubbed seals and cringe. "And why are you drinking *fat*?"

"The sea doesn't have lard. It *be* lard. And I drink 'cause it's pure ambrosia."

"No, that's not right. Seas aren't made of lard."

The captain furrows his brows as facial features collapse momentarily into one big wrinkle. "Then pray tell what they be."

"Uh, water."

"What be *water*?"

Your brain has been through too much already. You decide to let the question pass.

"No matter. This here isn't school, this be a pirate ship and on pirate ships we plunder things and hunt for treasure. Have ye plundered things before?"

"A bit."

"And have ye searched for treasure?"

"No, can't say that I have."

The captain smiles. "Worry not, me boy. 'Tis easy."

"I see, but how does Punk Rock fit into this?"

"Punk Rock?"

"Yeah. You like the Sex Pistols, right? And The Clash?"

"The Clash?"

"You only have a song title of theirs spray painted on your sails."

"If ye say we do, then we most certainly do."

You begin to worry about Piratebeard. But you realize he's old. Wouldn't be difficult to forget something as trivial as graffiti. Again, you let it pass. "So, are you going to teach me how to navigate the ship now?"

"We already have a navigator, matey."

"But the advertisement said you needed one."

The captain spends a moment in thought. "Perhaps we do. But let's not get all concerned about that. Let's go on a treasure hunt!"

Turn to page 79.

After what seems like an hour of climbing—with greasy sweat making your hands slippery on the chain rungs, sometimes pinching a piece of hand skin between metal rings—you come to the end of the ladder. Just hanging there, what seems like a mile off of the ground, the chain rope swaying gently in the wind.

You knock on the metal plate above you, looking for a hidden entrance, but there doesn't seem to be anything. The ladder doesn't appear to have a purpose.

Just hanging here for a while. You don't feel like climbing back down, yet there's no where else to go.

You call out for help:

"Is anybody in there?"

Knocking on the metal as hard as you can without slipping.

Hanging . . .

The sky is turning a dark blue and it's getting cold. The flabby waves have become white noise and your eyes are drooping shut . . .

"Where have you been?"

The voice nearly throws you from the ladder. You open your eyes and look around for him. Twenty feet up: a grubby ratty face grins down at you from an opening.

"The Captain's been waiting for you," says the weasel-ish pirate.

He throws down a rope ladder and you climb the rest of the way into the entrance of the ship. The inside is dark and smooth like flesh. Wires creep the walls like veins and the air is so hot and moist that you almost lose your balance.

The man before you is very small and sickly. His nose is thin and long and crooked and his teeth are sharp and gray. He looks similar to a classic pirate, with piercings, faded tattoos, a red bandana for a hat, and a peg leg. But he leaks some kind of brown beetle-fluid from his elbows.

"Eggy Joe," the man says, holding out his hand for an introduction.

You decide not to shake it.

Behind him stands some kind of man with wheels. He is about your size, leather clothing, chainmail suspenders. But his head is some kind of electronic device, like a stereo or computer. He's got large wheels instead of feet and small wheels on his wrists.

"We mustn't keep the White Rabbit waiting," says Eggy Joe.

He takes you through the wiry-flesh passageway. It feels like you are traveling down a throat. The ratty pirate oozes his rancid liquid on the ground like a trail to follow. You try to avoid the fluid, but sometimes your foot catches a drop and you slide, grasping a hunk of wall meat for balance. The electric-headed wheeler behind you slips nearly every three feet and thumps his hard computer head against your spine.

"White Rabbit?" you ask the leaky pirate.

"She's the Captain," says Eggy Joe. "The meanest bitch this larded ocean has ever seen."

Turn to page 23.

Confused, you allow the captain to lead you out of his office. Pirates didn't find treasure *before* their voyage, did they? Yet the ship is still in the harbor. It hasn't moved an inch.

"Come with me, boy," Piratebeard says. "Must round up me crew."

You nod, but your stomach ties up in knots. Further interaction with these people isn't your idea of fun, but you figure you'll have to accept their madness.

Piratebeard turns a corner, and there they are – flapping and insane pirates. How could such people organize a treasure hunt? You turn to the captain. He holds a megaphone. Piratebeard brings it to his lips and shouts:

"Avast ye scallywags! 'Tis time to quest for treasure! A copious bounty to those who succeed; a million lashes to all who fail!"

The pirates take note. Most sink to the floor and scurry about the deck on hands and knees. Others tip over lifeboats and crawl into them as though looking for something. A few rummage through their pockets. Some take off their clothes and shake them.

You turn from the spectacle. "What are they doing?"

"Why looking for treasure!"

"*On the ship?*"

Piratebeard gives you an odd look. "Of course. Where else does one look for treasure?"

"I don't know. An island, maybe?"

"No, me boy. That would be too much work, and we find all the treasure we need here on board. Why, there're new nuggets found each day!"

You nod. It feels like the safest thing to do. You turn back to the pirates. They have not let up.

"Open yer rotten maw!" one shouts.

The ancient pirate does as he is told.

"No! *Wider!*"

The pirate puts both hands in the guy's mouth and pulls. Something snaps. A broken jaw yawns wide.

"There we go! That's what I wanted to see!"

The shouter rams his hand down the other's throat. He digs around, ignoring the chunks that shoot up into his face.

"Ain't no treasure down thar!" He turns to the next pirate. "Hey! Open wide!"

A minute later: "Ain't nothing down here, either!"

Piratebeard hears this. "Then search yer quarters! I smell treasure all around! Loads of it!"

The pirates scamper away; the captain turns to you. He whispers under his breath: "But come, me boy. I've something special to show ye. Follow me to my bed-chamber."

Turn to page 84.

You decide to go south. There is a big "S" on the wall in front of you, so it must stand for south. Otherwise, there isn't any way of knowing which direction is which. You don't see a compass anywhere.

You start walking. The movements are difficult, like you are trudging through lard. You can feel the ship's electricity pouring into the ocean. Sometimes lightning explodes out of the cube and pierces the waves around you, as liquid electricity flows from the cabin on your head and streams down your chest.

After an hour of treading, you become desperate for a bathroom. You don't know where the bathrooms are on the ship nor do you know how to drop the anchor.

You hit the red button for help. It doesn't light up, so there's no way to tell if anyone is coming or not. You keep pressing it.

A few hours pass and your legs are getting sore. Blisters are forming in your shoes and your bladder is going through different stages of excruciating pain.

Frog Girl enters the room drinking meat from a straw.

"You need something?" she asks.

"I called for you three hours ago," your voice a whine. "I don't know how to stop."

"You need a break?" she asks.

You nod.

"Okay, take a break."

"I have to go to the bathroom."

"That's what those jugs are for," she points at jars dangling from the balance bars.

You didn't notice the jars before now.

"I've been needing to stop but I don't know how to drop anchor," you say.

Frog Girl reels the anchor down from the side of your head.

"You have control of it, you know," she says. "It is a part of your head now."

You are pissing in a jar and try to block her out for awhile. One jar fills and you go to another one. Then another one. The jars are overflowing onto the rubber floor.

After you are done: "Okay, let's give you a rest," Frog Girl twirling her long tongue at you.

Walking down the hallway with the anchor bouncing against your stomach, the chain pinching skin on your cheek . . .

"I'll show you to your bedroom," the girl says. "The cabin boy gets a very special room."

She takes you to a long hallway-like room with walls that shift and swirl like the insides of lava lamps. It is empty except for a bed that reminds you of a reclining electric chair.

Frog Girl lays you onto the chair/bed, stuffs your head into a cushy pillow package. She hooks the end of your anchor into some kind of lock and says, "So the ship doesn't move while you sleep."

You're not sure how the anchor could move with your head shoved tightly into a mold.

"Why are the walls moving?" you ask.

"To relax you. Your whole body feels like it is under the ocean. The wall's movement should even you out."

The toad girl pulls down her pants to expose dark green pubic hair and begins to unbutton your pants when you see the Captain through your ship's eyes stomping down the hallway toward your room. Frog Girl nearly rips your penis off when the Captain kicks down your door and screams, "What the hell is going on?"

Frog Girl leaps off of you and gets out of the Captain's way.

"We're heading North!" White Rabbit cries. "I told you to go South or West!"

"But I did go South. I walked toward the wall with the 'S.'"

"That doesn't stand for South! Why would it stand for South?"

The Captain paces your room. "If you weren't the cabin boy I would hang you."

"What's wrong?" you ask.

"Quiet," she says.

Her eyes close and she takes some deep breaths. You close

your eyes too.

"I'll be in my office," she says and you hear the click of her high-heeled shoes trail off down the hallway. "Don't raise anchor until I give you an order."

Frog Girl grinds one of your testicles.

"You've brought us into Zhotrax territory," she says. "Nobody ever comes back from Zhotrax territory."

Turn to page 69.

The captain's bedchamber isn't nearly as lush as his office. It's just a small, pink room with a frilly canopy bed as its focal point. A few stuffed animals rest on the comforter. An old, timeworn bear wears an eye-patch. A tattered bunny sports a peg leg. Above this, a pirate-themed boy band pouts seductively from a poster.

Though tiny, the room is filled with modern amenities: A big-screen plasma television churns out a DVD of Errol Flynn's *Captain Blood*. Nearer to the door, a barnacle-encrusted computer hums and flashes. Piratebeard steps in front of you and slams the monitor off. You don't have time to see what's on it.

"Nice room you have here." It's all you can think to say.

"That it is, that it is. But I didn't bring ye here to admire the décor." Captain Piratebeard walks to the bed and gets down on his hands and knees. He reaches between the floor and box spring and withdraws a gilded container three times the size of a shoebox. "I brought ye here to show off me special collection."

"Special collection of what?"

"Only the finest treasure found in ninety years at sea."

Images of gold and silver doubloons race through your head – flawless pearls and rare silks.

"Aye, priceless it is." Piratebeard grins. "And only I have the key."

You stare hungrily at the box. So many studded and jeweled inlays. It's probably worth a pretty penny even without the treasure inside. A part of you wants to bash Piratebeard with the closest heavy object. The treasure would be yours, but you couldn't stay onboard after braining the captain. You'd have to go ashore. And having treasure at the same time you're running from cops isn't safe.

You bite your lip and stay your hand.

Piratebeard inserts a long, ornate key into the lock. The box opens with a dry squeal. You can't wait to see what's inside. You crane your neck for a closer look and gag with revulsion. Eight golden turds line the box's interior. Some are so old that they've turned into powder.

"Dear sweet god!"

"Aye, me boy. Most are brown or green, but these are *gold!*"

You want to turn away, but your eyes remain glued to the absurdity. The turds aren't metallic, but have been spray-painted and spray-painted badly. Flecks of brown show through the cracking gold.

Piratebeard lifts two turds from the box. He rolls them around in his hand. "Did ye know I sleep with these? Aye, can't bear being away from me treasure!"

You cup your hand over your mouth, holding back bile.

"Often, ye find these in bedpans and chamber pots, but ye sometimes find them all over the ship." Piratebeard runs his fingers through golden powder. "Found this one in the scullery over twenty years ago. Lying atop the stove it was."

"On top of the stove!"

"Aye, and I've found treasure in stranger places, but I won't bore ye with sea tales. Not for now, at least."

You breathe a sigh of relief.

"But I do want to give ye something. Something special."

"Wait. You don't mean—"

Piratebeard selects a long, sticky specimen from the box. "I don't feel generous very often, but I like ye. Kinda look like me son, god rest 'em."

"Please, oh go no! Keep it!"

"But I insist." The captain walks toward you, the painted turd cupped in his outstretched hand. "Take it. I got plenty of treasure; it bothers me none."

"Just stay back! I don't want your treasure!" You pause. "My god, it stinks!"

"No need to be humble, me boy. And of course it stinks; *it's fresh.*"

If you tell the captain his treasure is shit, turn to page 116.

If you take the treasure, turn to page 39.

You are at a bridge that crosses over a lagoon between the island's upper thighs. Above you, the island's large vagina peers down like a god from Mount Olympus. A waterfall issues out of the opening, but you couldn't really call it a waterfall. It isn't water pouring out; it is a chunky river of animal fetuses. Pumping out of the island's vagina like the island is giving birth to millions upon millions of tiny baby creatures.

The bridge is not really a bridge, but a fallen log. The Captain has Saryn test it first.

"If the log breaks your wings will save you," White Rabbit says.

Saryn gets across fine. The log seems tightly bonded into the plastic hills. It doesn't shift at all.

The Captain goes next. Then Trapface and Tendon.

Now it is your turn. You hesitate. You don't know why, but your gut is telling you not to step foot on that log.

White Rabbit orders you across, but your feet aren't moving.

If you refuse to climb onto the log, turn to page 65.
If you obey the Captain, turn to page 131.

You keep your eyes open. Piratebeard will surely reach for your package or stick something unyielding up your ass if you give him the chance.

But the pirates. Their eyes are all closed. And not one of them has moved an inch since entering Satan's Mullet.

And things seem a little different now. A little more swimmy. A little more swirley. Floorboards suddenly breathe. The ceiling vibrates as the entire room hums. All in all, it's not so bad. The special effects are actually kind of neat. They remind you of the acid you did back in high school.

Soon, you have a full-blown body buzz. Electrical currents ride up and down your spine in waves. The feeling is almost sensual. You get lost in the moment. Your hands play over your body. The tingling: *sensational*. You close your eyes and watch tiny pinpricks of color morph into complex fractal patterns.

Then a rattling sound distracts you. You open your eyes. Your phallus engorges. Newly found timbers quiver inside you. The pirates – they have all become hot, nubile women. They rub their backs against polls and make oohing and aahing sounds. Most wear Amazon-looking outfits. Others, however, are completely nude. A techno album plays somewhere in the background as one of the ladies bends down to snort a fat line from a handheld mirror.

This is some party. Satan's Mullet is a happening place— perhaps the most happening place on the Sea of Lard. You can't believe Piratebeard told you to close your eyes.

You walk over to one of the girls—and then realize that, once you leave Satan's Mullet, she'll turn back into a grizzled, man-hungry pirate.

To hell with it. This is too good to miss.

You stand beside one of the ladies. Her eyes are like blue saucers of sex. You try the standard pick-up line:

"Hey, baby—wanna mercy-fuck?"

She giggles. There's something in her eyes, but you're not sure what it is. You've never seen that sort of look on a woman's face before. Well, you've seen it in movies, but never in real life.

It looks like lust, pure and simple.

But your pockmarked face, crooked nose, and thin, patchy hair aren't attractive features. Most ladies grimace when they see you. Some point, and others whisper to their friends. But this woman, she's different. She sees something that others miss – though you're not certain what that *something* is.

She looks down at your package. Her eyes widen.

"Packing heat, ja?" She massages your underwear bulge with long, perfectly formed fingers. "Excited, no?"

The German accent turns you on. "Oh yes. *Very* excited."

"Und Sie vant *blow*?" She whispers in your ear. "Ich habe lots auf candy."

"Oh yeah. Lay it out."

The woman opens a ring on her finger. The stone is hollow and filled with fine white powder. You snort the contents as the woman starts some lesbian shit with an ex-pirate.

The other woman is less attractive, a little pudgy around the edges. But what the hell— the show's free.

"Tongue mich!" the first woman moans, pointing at her crotch. "Tongue mich hier! *Ich muß gefühl dich!*"

You didn't realize a tongue could slide into so many places.

The woman turns to you. Her eyes roll back in ecstasy. Beads of sweat drip down her chest. Still, she manages to purr: "But Sie sind a bad little mench." She pauses to let her friend massage her breasts. "Herr Piratebeard besagt *close ihre augen*, no?"

You're confused as to why this sexy little thing would care what a pirate says. Ignoring her question, you get in on the action.

You grab her ass with both hands. Then you ram your tongue deep down her friend's throat.

Wait . . . something wiggles down there. And the first woman's butt feels all crinkly and weird.

You withdraw your tongue. Squirmy things cover it.

Maggots.

Gagging with revulsion, you spit them onto the floor. You look up at the first woman and piss your briefs. She shambles forward, her face a decaying ruin. The second woman—she's a denuded skeleton. Thin, parchment-like skin clings to yellow bones. Just below her, another living corpse lies thrashing on the floor. Its stick-like limbs are so fragile that one breaks off.

You unleash a scream, and scream again as you realize there's more than just three. Hundreds of marble-like eyes stare through you, seeing nothing.

A steaming cauldron also sits on the floor, filled with something that smells like a mixture of semen and feces. Looming above it, a fleshy red thing stirs and stirs. An identical creature squats on a shelf lined with human heads. The entity doesn't have to speak to condemn you. Just one look at it causes all the pain and anguish you've wrought to swirl back ten-fold.

You glance down at your hand and scream again. Tendons are visible through holes in mottled gray skin. You bring your palms to your face. Your index finger falls into the hole where your nose had been. Ragged fingernails tear soft and tattered flesh. Something wet and orb-like clings to your cheek. You feel the connecting cord and realize it's your eye.

Finally, you smell yourself. It's a sickly-sweet green/brown odor. You want to vomit, but your stomach is too desiccated.

A black, wrought-iron door swings open. Captain Piratebeard enters the room. His skull is capped by twin devil horns. His eyes are cat-like and glowing. No longer wrapped in pirate gear, the captain sports a full-body cape made of human flesh. Assorted body parts cling to it, held in place by thick black stitches. Arms, legs, and teeth – all disconnected, all moving. The cloak moans through two pairs of lips.

"Welcome to forever, me boy!" The captain's teeth are sharp and green. "Now it be time to stick a flamin' pitchfork up yer ass!"

Piratebeard brings just that out from behind his back. He advances. You want to close your eyes. You wish you had listened to

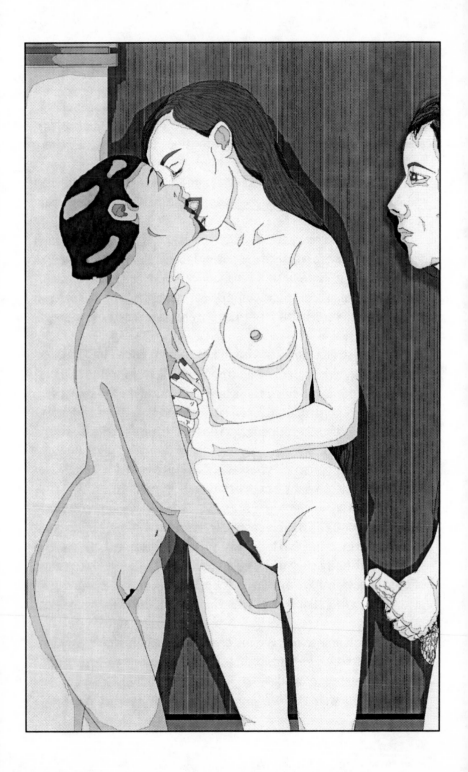

the captain when he was still human. But once your eyes have been opened, they can never again be closed.

THE END

You scream and wave your arms around, but the demonic faerie is too far away. She doesn't seem to hear or see you. But you don't give up, thrashing your body around and screaming until your throat cracks.

Then your body explodes out of the lard as an enormous whale/turtle surfaces with you on top of it. The creature's spiky green head turns all the way around like an owl until it faces you on its back. It opens its mouth and lets out a deep groan.

Tentacles rip out of the sea and swing across the turtle shell at you. Trying to dodge the creature's octopus limbs, you slip on the greasy surface and are easily captured. The tentacles slide you across the shell toward its soggy gaping maw.

You can feel the heat from its throat as a woman falls out of the sky and flops on the shell in front of you. It is one of the demonic faeries, coated in chunks of fat from the ocean. She stands and slashes at the tentacles with a saber, freeing you, and she screams, "Get the grease off my wings."

You stand up and approach her.

"Hurry!" she cries, as she fights the whale/turtle's enormous jaws and limbs.

Her black butterfly wings seem so delicate that you're afraid to touch them. But you rub them gently, slowly brushing the oil away. Before you get a chance to finish, she whips around and grabs you in her tattooed arms. Then launches off into the air.

She can't fly very well. Her wings still wet and you are heavier than she is. You wonder why she doesn't just drop you and save herself.

"What was that thing?" you ask.

The woman keeps flying. She takes you deep into the sweaty sky, her eyes set on a small piece of land on the horizon.

Turn to page 54

"Oh yes." You briefly consider the oddity of spearheading an insurrection in your undies. "I got a bounty down there. Sure do."

His eyes gleam. "That's the spirit, me boy! And to think I thought ye were a cold fish!"

Piratebeard reaches into your briefs. Warty hands envelope you. The captain's eyes explode. Blood shoots from his ears. His hair catches fire. His tongue swells, turns blue, and then melts away along with his facial features.

Eyes darting, you expect chaos—but the other pirates don't seem concerned over the noisy demise of their captain.

"Holy mackerel!" one shouts. "That must be some willy ye got thar!"

"Yeah!" screams another. "Lemme see!"

The pirates converge, stepping over Piratebeard's flaming corpse. They cover you in seconds, fingers kneading. You bat most away, but a few slip past your flailing hands and touch the electric gadget. Their deaths don't stop others from trying to do the same.

Salvatore/Timmy bursts through the door. His shouts end the melee.

"Damn all of you, get up! Captain Tonydanza's gone, and we no longer rut like pigs!"

The pirates pull away. You sprint to the cabin boy. "Oh god, you don't know how happy I am to see you! I almost got gang raped by a hundred pirates!"

Salvatore/Timmy grins expansively. "And I am happy to see you, too. You see, my personal protocol stipulates that I cannot kill humans—but it doesn't say I can't have others do the job for me."

Personal protocol? *Kill humans*?

"Now that the captain's out of the way, I control the ship." He grins again. "Time to steer it towards *destiny*."

You feel as though you might have made a mistake.

Salvatore/Timmy's voice adopts a flat, monotonic cadence. "The human race will be exterminated." He bleeps. "But you shall be spared."

You blubber.

"I'll make you *bleep* like me." The cabin boy rips at his face. Skin peels away like latex. You scream at the flashing, robotic head hiding beneath.

"For I am *Kuntis Mechanus*, footsoldier and spy for *King Robotis III*. Your race is slated for *beep* death once the mothership transforms this pile of useless lumber into something more suitable. It would be foolish to maintain your *bleep* present form."

If you decline, turn to page 95.
If you accept the evil alien robot's offer, turn to page 152.

"I can't. I just can't. This is too much. I just want to go home. I just want to leave this place. Oh god, I don't even care if I go to jail!"

Kuntis Mechanus says nothing, but the blinking diode in the middle of his face looks pissed. Metal pinchers grab you and lift your body a foot off the floor. They squeeze your ribs hard, so hard that you feel you'll break bones if you breathe too deeply.

The ex-cabin boy transports you to the deck on red shiny wheels. You continue until you reach a door near the sleeping chamber. *Kuntis Mechanus* wills the hinges open. The smell that rushes out to greet you is as bad as the one in the bilge. It's a different sort of stench, though.

"Please, don't!" You plead. "I—I want to become a robot!"

"Too late!" he bleeps, wheeling into the room. Pinchers recoil, and you fall to the floor. *Kuntis Mechanus* rolls backward quickly. The door slams and locks in less than a second.

You pick yourself up. You can see little, but it appears as though the chamber is littered with baggy white blobs. They squish as you step on them.

You bend down to pick one up. It feels like it's made of plastic. You grope around inside. Something wet and chunky slides across your fingers. Bringing the digits to your nose, you gag. It smells like shit.

Then you realize it smells like shit because it *is* shit. You're holding one of a thousand used adult diapers.

You beat your fists against the wall. You scream until your throat bleeds. You're going to be locked in here forever, doomed to die amongst pirate waste. There's nothing to eat. Nothing to eat unless . . .

But no, that's unthinkable.

If you choose to live off shit, turn to page 172.
If you choose not to, this is . . .
THE END

You wake up in an electric chair-like bed that has your head locked into a pillow. The walls are shifting around you in a heart-pulsing manner. Like you are inside someone's lung cavity.

"He's awake," you hear somebody say.

Frog Girl and Eggy Joe are hovering over you. White Rabbit standing off to the side.

"We were worried about you," Eggy Joe says. "Froggy even thought you'd gone into a coma."

"We would have had to cut off your head so somebody else could pilot the ship," Frog Girl says.

The Captain opens the door and shines light into your eyes.

"Bring him to the helm immediately," she says as she click-stomps out of the room on her high white heels.

Eggy Joe nods and gets you to your feet.

At the helm, you survey the damage with your ship's eyes.

"Not much," you tell the Captain. "A few bumps inside, some overturned crates, a lot of mess."

You look through your external ship's eyes and see the ocean is no longer made of lard. Instead, it is made of some other type of meat material. Dead chunks of flesh floating in a mess of blood. And your body feels submerged in the gore.

"There's something different about the ocean," you say. "It's made of . . ."

"Animal fetuses," Eve says, entering the room.

The Captain slides the back of her hand down the demonic faerie's cheek.

Eve says, "Pig fetuses, mostly. But some are human. Some are cow, elephant, bear. And other animals I didn't recognize."

"The entire ocean is some kind of giant embryonic soup," you tell them.

Eve continues, "The whirlpool took us into another world where the ocean is not lard."

"Impossible," the Captain says.

Eve crimps her butterfly wings. "There are secret worlds everywhere."

You see land out of your western ship's eye.

"There's some kind of island out there," you say.

The Captain raises her eyebrow tattoo.

"It's strange. It's shaped like a . . ." you try concentrating on that eye. "I think it's a . . . vagina."

The Captain's eyes light up. She turns to Eve, "Do you think?"

"I'll go check," Eve says, and leaves the room.

The Captain twists the side of your head until the anchor is raised.

"Move in for a closer look," she says. "If it really is cunt-shaped, we'll want to land there."

You begin slushing the ship through the fetus gumbo toward the island.

"Legend has it," the Captain says, "that hundreds of years ago, there lived a ruthless pirate named Pussycat who hid her treasure in the womb of a cunt-shaped island."

You get closer and can see that it is definitely a vagina. There is even a small jungle that looks like its pubic hair.

"She was the richest of all pirates," White Rabbit continues. "Even to this day, no one has accumulated more wealth than the great Pussy. If this is the island, we will all live like kings for the rest of our lives."

Drawing closer, you can see almost every detail of the vagina-island ahead of you. It looks very lifelike, perhaps even made of flesh and hair instead of rock and jungle.

You enter a school of enormous bubbles. Actually, more like pods. They are made of skin with pulsing veins, hovering over the ocean from what looks to be tendons that stretch down from webby rain clouds. There is movement inside of them. Perhaps they are very large wombs. Instead of containing infants, perhaps they contain fully grown adults.

"What do you see?" the Captain asks.

"Floating wombs," you tell her.

"Wombs?"

The ship collides with one of the flesh bubbles and it pops, releasing a swarm of bees.

You tell her, "They're filled with bees."

"Bees!"

The buzzing insects tornado around the ship, some of them stinging the hull but do no damage. They don't hurt you, but you can feel their stingers going into the box on your head. You pop another bubble and release another swarm of bees.

A woman's voice comes on the intercom: "Captain, come to your office immediately."

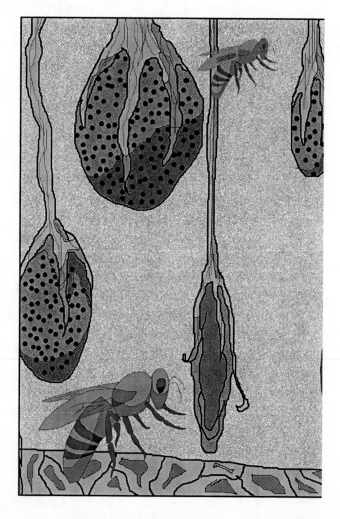

White Rabbit lowers the anchor on your head and has you come upstairs with her. You see her first lieutenant, Eve, lying dead on the desk of her office. Her sisters and Pussy Rot standing around her.

"What happened?" the Captain screams.

"She was in the crow's nest," they say.

The Captain picks a dead bee out of her black butterfly wing. There are dead bees all over her. It isn't really a bee, but some kind of metal robot. White Rabbit pulls a stinger out. It is three inches long.

"They aren't poisonous," a lieutenant says. "They are like small daggers that break off under the skin."

White Rabbit drops the bee and it shatters on the ground. Mostly hollow inside.

"They are traps," she says. "This must be the island. Pussycat's island is riddled with traps like these. If we'd been on an old-fashioned sailboat we would all be dead right now."

The Captain wraps around one of the demon faeries, digging her plastic head into the girl's ratty-haired neck.

"Kumi," she says, a sturdy yet sad voice. "You're my right arm now."

Her eye goes to another of the girls. "Said, you're my left."

"Bury her in the lower decks," the Captain says as she pulls you out of the room. "But make sure not to wake the dead down there."

White Rabbit has you walk as close as you can get to the island, avoiding as many bee bubbles as possible. But almost every bubble you come across pops with ease against the jagged metal ship. Probably a dozen swarms are trailing behind you.

You lower the anchor onto the underwater parts of the vagina-island, which you imagine to be the thighs of a giantess. And wait for the bees to sting themselves to death against the hull or get bored and fly away. Most of them do not fly away.

The Captain calls the crew together to form a party to raid the island's womb. She says her lieutenants Kumi and Said will lead the party, and wants four volunteers to accompany them.

If you want to volunteer, turn to page 143.
If you don't want to volunteer, turn to page 118.

You run around the deck, looking for a way down while trying to avoid the cabin boy. Finally, you see a dark, gaping hole near the rear of the ship. Rickety wooden steps extend into blackness. The place is cold and dark and more than a little scary, but if the bilge is anywhere, you assume it's down here.

You descend the steps for what feels like ages. The case shouldn't be this long. Too much time passes before you find yourself inside a narrow wooden hallway. Torches fastened to the wall provide the only illumination. You look around. Everything seems musty, ancient, and *deep*. The light at the stairwell's mouth looks like a pinprick.

Footsteps sound. They seem to be coming from the end of the hall. You strain your eyes, but can't see more than twenty feet in front of you. The torches don't provide enough illumination.

You take off running. Your steps echo hollow, like you're sprinting through a cave. Just when you feel you're about to catch up a door squeals, and the steps vanish.

Pausing where you think the sounds ended, you see that you stand near the hall's end. There are only two doors here, one on each side.

You open the door to your left. Inside, a small group of pirates lay coiled in supplication beneath a rickety old chair elevated by at least twenty phonebooks. A scrawled banner above the chair exclaims HAPIE 100rd BURFHDEI CEPTI'N PERITEBAERT!

But the man in the chair isn't Piratebeard. The man in the chair has been dead so long that his skin has bloated and blackened. Those in attendance don't seem to notice as they variously intone both Piratebeard's and Merdelan's name.

You close the door quickly.

Piratebeard has to be inside the room to your right. You throw open the door. The slaughterhouse smell hits you first.

You vomit for a minute, then dry-heave for a minute more. The room brims with corpses. Dead people with mohawks, leather jackets, and dangling chains lay on the floor. Smears of decomposition conceal anarchy tattoos and facial piercings. The bodies appear to have lain there for weeks.

Above it all, Captain Piratebeard stands.

"Oh hello, me boy! Couldn't wait to dance for me, could ye? Had to go and find yer old captain?" He looks down at the corpses. "Sorry about the mess. I just stuck them in here until I could find a better place for 'em."

You stutter wordlessly.

"Didn't expect me to just sit around after me boys and I escaped from that blasted old pirates home, did ye? I yearned for a ship! Couldn't sail out on me ass."

You don't know what to do. Should you go back to Salvatore/Timmy and agree to help overthrow this murderer? But the cabin boy threatened to fuck you and your non-existent family. And what if he was in on it, too?

Maybe you should just play along. Pretending that nothing's wrong has helped you in the past.

Or maybe you should do the unthinkable. Maybe you should tell Piratebeard your dark secret, make him feel as though you're as bad a person as he. If you do that, perhaps he won't make you join the dead punks in this dark and horrible room.

If you tell Piratebeard you're a child molester, turn to page 110.
If you run back to Salvatore/Timmy, turn to page 126.
If you pretend nothing's wrong, turn to page 166.

You accept with great reservations.

And Captain Piratebeard obliges, stripping you to your briefs as members of his crew hold you down. He chains your flailing body to the base of the *papier mache* wheel. Calloused and warty digits paint strange symbols onto your chest.

Piratebeard intones: "Oh Merdelan, Satan of the Seas, bestow upon this initiate your dark blessing. Allow him to drink from your cup of brine. Allow him to eat of your belly of scales."

You struggle against your bonds while pirates spasm on the floor. The scene reminds you of the scary, backwoods church your grandma took you to when you were young. Luckily, there are no serpents this time.

Piratebeard turns his back to you. In one hand, he holds aloft a golden chalice. In the other, a shiny dagger sparkles. "Pass this vessel, and, with blade in hand, drain into it a pleasing offering."

The pirates stop gyrating long enough to pass the chalice and the dagger. One after the other, they nick their wrists. Blood mixes with blood in the cup. Someone gets confused and pisses in the chalice. Another just spits.

Once it has completed its round, the cup is returned. You look at the vile mixture and gag.

Piratebeard places his hand on your shoulder. "Worry not," he says. "Merdelan will protect ye from VD."

You drink the stuff. The first taste makes you convulse. Piratebeard covers your mouth with his hand and presses hard. You can't spit it out. Fluid slides down your throat in a warm trail.

Piratebeard watches you, a look of rapture lighting his face. "*Praise Merdelan! Praise Merdelan! Praise Merdelan!*"

Your belly grows warmer each time he says that name. The warmth soon spreads until it centers itself in your back. Heat gives way to pain. Agony waves ripple across your spine. You fear your organs have suddenly come alive and are trying to make a break for it.

"Yes, me boy. Push! *Push!*"

You push. Your back feels like it's either defecating or about

to drop a fetus. Sweat beads on your forehead. You almost swallow
your flapping tongue.

Then something pops. The sound is wet and juicy.

Piratebeard beams. "Ah, matey, those are a fine set of timbers!" He holds up a mirror whose handle looks like a bronzed, demonic cock. "Have a look!"

You avert your eyes. You don't want to see the horror sprouting
in shimmery currents from your back. "How—how do I get them
back in?"

He smiles. "Just will them inside, me boy. And, when ye want
to flare them, just shout *shiver me timbers!*"

You concentrate hard. Moments later, what feels like a thousand huge spaghetti strands slide into your back.

Piratebeard unties you from the wheel. You not only feel like a
mutant, you also feel *raped.*

"Can I get dressed? *Please.*"

The captain makes a *tut-tut* sound.

"What does that mean!"

"Lost yer clothes, I did. Don't know where they could've
gone."

"But you said you were omnipotent!"

His eyes sparkle. "Omnipotent about everything but that."

"Can you give me something else to wear?"

"Afraid not. All we have are the clothes on our backs."

Your eyes dart across the pirate-strewn floor. "I'm going to
have to spend the rest of my time here in underwear! *With these
people!*"

Piratebeard's mouth waters. "Aye, me boy. Aye, aye, aye."

"No, Captain! Please, no! Oh god!"

The captain pretends not to hear. "But ye got yer timbers
now. Enough ritual! Let's go out and do pirate-things!"

Piratebeard escorts you out, his hand positioned just above
your ass.

Turn to page 28.

You call out, but the ship's crew is nowhere to be seen. It is like a ghost ship, phantom-hypnotic with ugly fruit growing from barbed wire.

You call out again. No answer. Perhaps they are wandering filthy-clothed through Pirate Town. Perhaps the sea is not really water but some kind of ooze-creature as big as the landscape.

On the next call, somebody answers. You don't understand the person, but there definitely was some kind of a response given. Like a muffled voice.

You call again.

Wait a minute.

The voice responds. A feminine echoing. But the words are not right. Like someone speaking backwards. You call out again and follow the voice twenty feet to your left, finding a large hole in the ship covered in stringy mold. The woman's voice echoes out of the hole. You think you understand her, like she is speaking English words, but you can't comprehend them.

The hole is like a cave with metal stalagmites and stalactites. Lard waves splat against the side of the ship underneath you as you climb through the greasy hole, crab-walking into jagged darkness.

There is some light and movement up ahead. The voice echoes at you again, this time more of a screechy noise than a woman's voice. You find yourself inside a room of garbage and metal scraps, lit by a single lightbulb dangling from the ceiling.

A woman is lying in a pool of muck here, integrated into the debris. Oily bubbles spill out of her mouth like words and she flaps a fishy tail at you.

A mermaid.

Or something like a mermaid. Her upper half is a woman's and her lower half is like a sea serpent. Long spiny tail three times your size, coiled through nails and sewage. She tries to move toward you but she is trapped under metal pieces and wrapped up in maybe a mile of razor wire. The wire cutting through her scales, large bloody gashes that smell like rotten fish.

She whines. Dark, sad eyes at you. She has locks of sea

weed for hair, shiny emerald nipples.

Her fishy eyes are alluring. They pull you inside of them, put you in a trance. The next thing you know you are up to your knees in putrid glue, trying to free the fishy woman from the razor wire. Her scales glossy on your fingers. You become sticky with her blood.

She sniffs at your hair as you work on the wires, and licks her blood off of you.

"What am I doing?" you ask yourself, and you watch her blink at you with shark eyes.

After you loosen the wires around the creature, she begins to wiggle. Slithers and reaches out with her arms like she thinks she is free. Only to tighten the wires back onto her body.

A banshee shriek fills the cave and she thrash-struggles her body and tail in a panic. She takes you with her. The enormous serpent tail knocking you off your feet and into the slime, flailing on you until you become wrapped in the razor wire with her, hooking ripping into your skin. She rolls you together, through sharp metal cereal.

You feel like a peeled lemon by the time she calms. Trapped under her and tight to her fishy-fleshed body. She rests her face into your neck. Her tears are warm and comforting, and make you day-dream.

Moments of deep breathing. Your breaths in sync with hers. You feel her naked breasts against you. Hard nipples poking through your soggy clothes. With wriggling fingers, you pull your shirt up to your neck so her breasts can press against your bare chest. Your breathing goes out of rhythm with hers as an erection breaks through a tear in your pants and digs into her dried scales, itchy and rough against your cock.

She feels it against her and lifts her head to face you with cold black eyes.

Just staring at you.

Then she opens her mouth and presses it against your neck. Her tongue is forked like a snake when she slips it under your chin, over your lips. Her body squirms into your cock, trying to get it inside

of her. But you have no idea where her cunt is or if she even has one at all. Her breath is hot wax on you.

Your penis finds moist scales underneath her. Not a vagina but much better than the dried itchy flesh. She frenzy-rubs you, your skin cutting into the razor wire and shedding against chunks of metal. You see her wounds open larger. Fresh blood dripping into the gray muck, but she doesn't care. She pulses until you cum against each other, her squeals like a dolphin's. And then she collapses her head, your face buried in her twisted hair as you go to sleep.

When you awake, she is dead on top of you.

You find her vagina under some scales and cum inside of her again. But it isn't the same. The fishy scent coating your lungs and face is getting rotten.

For some reason, you don't attempt to free yourself. Even though she is dead and decomposing you don't want to leave her. As if she still has you in some kind of trance.

You die facing her, staring into her dried-goop eyes.

Glued to them. Trapped inside of them.

THE END

When you return to the mess hall, you see that Captain Piratebeard has retaken his seat. In his hand, he holds a severed foot cut from one of the bilge bodies.

"Took ye long enough!" he calls. "Got that extra-special something, too!"

You shiver, knowing that you'll soon be touching that green, bony thing.

"Picked the best specimen, I did." He drops the foot into your hand and orders that you rub it all over your body.

You do so, gagging.

Just behind you, a pirate wearing a pink pointy bra and panties lifts a bagpipe to his mouth. Hellish cacophony pours out.

"According to *The Book of Merdelan*, all footdances must be accompanied by bagpipes and lots of fevered groping! Now wave that foot in the air and sashay this way!"

Piratebeard pretends that he's thrown a rope over you and is gradually reeling you in. You play his game. Your body twists and buckles. You wave the foot as though it were a baton. Once you get close enough, the captain runs his index finger down your chest.

"Aye, nice! But I bet ye got something nicer a little farther south!"

With this other hand, he grabs the front of your briefs and stretches them open.

The bagpipes scream louder. You can barely hear Piratebeard above the racket. "Let's see if ye got a bounty in thar!"

The captain is about to die. You've never killed anyone before.

A touch of nerves—and guilt—sets in.

Do you stop the captain? If so turn to page 128.
If not, turn to page 93.

You decide to tell Piratebeard your secret. It's something you've revealed to no one.

You steady yourself, breathing heavily. Then you let it fly: "I'm a child molester."

Piratebeard furrows his brows. "What did ye just say, me boy?"

"I said I'm a child molestor. I molest children."

"A child molestor, eh." He pauses. "That means ye get yer jollies off with the kiddies, right?"

"Basically."

"I see."

Relief floods in. It seems your plan may have worked. "So, you shouldn't worry about me knowing your secret because—now—you know mine."

"I don't mind ye knowin' about the bodies. They're boring. They don't do much. Besides, I'm above the petty laws of man." Piratebeard pauses. "But, for the life of me, I can't figure out what made ye think I'd be cozy with a child molester!"

The captain's tone blasts away any relief you might've felt.

"People who do that to wee young'uns should be deballed and thrown to flesh-eating walruses. *The Book of Merdelan* commands nothing less. But I have different ways of dealing with such folk."

Piratebeard shouts "*Shiver me timbers!*" An instant later, glistening pirate appendages writhe and pulse.

You try to run, but a timber shoots forth, ensnarling you. One shoves itself in your mouth, filling it like a cock. Another slides into your ass. It branches out inside your intestines, splitting them, spewing fecal matter inside your body cavity. Another wraps itself around the top of your scrotum, squeezing tighter and tighter until balls detach.

Piratebeard laughs. "Now ye know how those kiddies feel, me boy—but I'm not done with ye yet!"

The timbers vibrate inside you. The sensation is by no means erotic. It feels as though your essence is being sucked away with a straw. Your face dries and then caves in. The rest of your body follows suit. Finally your bones become powder as everything is drawn up into the timbers and then into Piratebeard himself.

The captain retracts his timbers. He removes the demon-cock mirror from his coat pocket. Looking into it, Piratebeard admires the latest addition to his pirate beard.

THE END

"I'll have the meatloaf," you tell Pussy Rot.

"It'll take about twenty minutes," she says.

"Fine," you say.

Waiting for the food.

An alarm goes off.

"Zhotrax ships approaching," a voice says over the intercom.

So you run upstairs to the helm and hit White Rabbit on her way down.

"Hurry! Hurry!" she screams at you.

She raises your anchor and pushes you as hard as she can. But before you make it to the helm, a hole opens up in the ceiling and down comes a large muscled humanoid with a squid-beard and a crab-like body. He draws his saber and swings it at the Captain. She claws at him and backs you away, cutting into his beard with her electric fingernails, but another appears out of the stairwell and before you can give her warning her head is cut from her neck and lands on the floor next to you. Sparks and wires squirming out of the neck.

You try to call for help, but before a word can come out your own head is chopped off at the neck. And as your severed head falls to the floor, the entire ship sinks deep into the ocean of lard.

THE END

You leave the cave and wait outside the entrance for the others to come out with the treasure. Their footsteps echo at you.

Above you, there is silver netting that stretches from the trees across the top of the vagina, like fishnet panties. You didn't notice it before, but it covers the entire sky around you. The path you took was the only opening through the netting.

It is moving slightly, but there is no wind. You peer across, looking for the source of the movement. Up a trail, alongside the inner labia, you see Kumi the missing demon faerie girl entangled in the net. Like a black butterfly trapped in a spider's web. She is struggling, fighting to break free.

You call into the cave for help, your voice echoing in the darkness.

There is no response.

Kumi sees you and cries out, but you don't know what you can do. She is only about twenty feet off the ground. Perhaps you can climb up to her.

You only get about three steps off the ground when the box on your head gets caught on part of the netting. You reach your arm up to free it, but when your hand touches the net it becomes glued. Then the rest of your body sticks to the net, as you notice a clear adhesive fluid leaking out of the silvery fabric.

A spider's web.

You panic. Your head is locked tight against the webbing. You get one of your sticky hands free and then drop onto your weight. Gravity allows you to free most of your body, but the cabin on your head won't release.

There is only one thing to do: take the cabin off. You loosen the straps on your face and pull, but the large needle inside of your brain seems to be hooked.

You push against the cabin as hard as you can. There is ripping and cracking, then you hit the ground ... minus the top of your skull.

It reminds you of carving a pumpkin. The lid of the jack-olantern still attached to the cabin in the web, with stringy meat dangling from it. Your open head leaks pumpkin chowder onto the plastic, as you stare up into the air.

The last thing you see is an enormous metal spider on top of a butterfly, digging its fangs into her belly.

It begins to rain an inky fluid.

Ants are making a home inside of your head.

THE END

There's no way in hell you're going to handle gold painted shit. Besides, the thought of cutting the old coot down to size gives you a thrill. You're sick of his games; they have to stop. Otherwise, you'll go cackle-cackle mad before the voyage even begins.

"That's not treasure, Captain. That's shit!"

Piratebeard blinks. "What say ye, me boy?"

"Your treasure is from someone's ass."

He shakes his head back and forth. "No!"

"You've painted it gold. That's all."

"Not true!"

"Just look at it! *Smell* it!"

Piratebeard bites the end of the turd. "See! 'Tis *pure!*"

"Please don't do that again!"

The captain waves his treasure in your face. "Ye bite it if ye believe me not!"

Disgusted, you slap the thing out of his hand. It smacks the wall with a wet *thunk*. Piratebeard watches his treasure fall to pieces on the floor. He stands for a few seconds, motionless. Then his shoulders sag and his eyes water.

"Sweet Merdelan, ye're right."

"Of course I am."

"'Tis shite." His hands claw at his face. "After all these years . . . *just shite!*"

You walk over to Captain Piratebeard. You've purposely devastated the guy, but it still hurts to see him in pain. Guilt tugs at you. You drape your arm over him, and he sinks into your embrace.

"It's okay, Captain."

His tears stain your sleeve. "No, 'tis not okay. Will never be okay again."

"It will be. I mean that."

He looks at you. His eyes seem like those of a hurt child. "Really?"

"Really."

The old man smiles. A gnarly hand plays over your crotch.

You hear your zipper slide down.

"*Captain Piratebeard*!"

"Come on, me boy. Be an old pirate's treasure. Make him feel seaworthy again."

You pull away before Piratebeard can breech your underwear.

The captain's face folds into a grimace. "You dare rebuke me?"

"But—"

His teeth glisten like daggers. "No one rebukes Captain Piratebeard!"

The captain's lunatic grin tells you that you're no longer safe. You back away, but not far enough to escape Piratebeard's reach. He unsheathes his sword and, with a bestial groan, rams it through one side of your head and out the other.

The last thing you feel before you die: warty hands unfastening your belt.

If you want to know what happens to your corpse, turn to page 142. If that doesn't interest you, it's . . .

THE END

The four volunteers are Lox, Frog Girl, Eggy Joe, and Studio. They go with Kumi and Said once the metal bees no longer pose a threat. Frog Girl smacking her long tongue against your butt with giggles as she leaves the room.

You follow them with your external ship's eyes as they take a rowboat out on the fetus soup. They land on the beach and appear smaller than crickets. Then you don't see them anymore.

Hours pass and you still don't see them.

The rest of the day goes by. Nothing.

"We're going out in the morning," the Captain tells you as Pussy Rot feeds you corn cakes in the kitchen. "It's going to be more dangerous than I thought."

At dawn, you arrive on the beach, your legs coated in blood and womb juices. The island is made out of a shiny plastic material, but it doesn't seem artificial to you. Perhaps it only seems natural because the embryonic ocean is so repugnant in comparison.

"Can you see *any* of them?" White Rabbit asks.

Pubic hairs blowing in the wind.

"I see them," Saryn says from above you, fluttering around like a butterfly.

She lands and walks the group to the edge of the pubic hair jungle.

They are all dead. Their bodies lying between the trees with their skulls blown apart. Brain and blood in messy pools across the ground.

"It's like their heads exploded out of their necks," Pussy Rot says.

"Don't go near them," the Captain says. "It's some kind of trap."

You only count five bodies. There should be six of them.

"Somebody's missing," you say.

The Captain examines the corpses. "Kumi's not among them.

She might still be alive somewhere on the island. We'll have to look for her."

But you need to find a way around the pubic hair . . .

"The jungle *is* avoidable," Saryn tells White Rabbit. "There's a bald spot near the lower portion of the island's outer labia."

"Can we get there?" White Rabbit asks.

"I think so," Saryn says.

White Rabbit nods. "Lead the way."

Turn to page 86.

You take the salmon jerky and orange and bring it back to the helm. After eating the little snack, you feel refreshed and ready to get moving again. The Captain hasn't given you any orders yet, but you figure you should go in the opposite direction of the "S" on the wall. So you raise the anchor and begin to move in the opposite direction. This time you jog instead of walk, trying to get out of this dangerous area as quick as possible.

Out of the back of your head, through a ship eye, you see several spiky pirate ships heading in your direction. So you start running. The emergency sirens and lights make you jump, but you keep moving as quick as you can. The Captain bursts into the room with heavy breaths and utters something like "Praise the saints," but you don't understand why she would say that. She runs onto the treadmill floor beside you, and runs in place next to you, pushing you to move faster.

"We can make it," she says. "Just don't slow down."

Lightning explodes from all sides of the cube as you rip through the lard, moving at top speed.

Then something strikes you through the back of the head. A cannonball. It has punctured a hole in the ship. Smoke and sparks are coming out of you and fill the room.

You become dizzy with pain. It feels like a bullet is lodged in your skull.

"Don't worry about that," White Rabbit says. "Just keep going. Ignore the pain. Concentrate on running."

You can feel cannonballs splashing all around you, but none of them hit. Soon you are far ahead of the pirate army. The Captain has you change course and head southwest. Slow to a jog. An hour passes and you return to walking speed, catching your breath.

"Who were they?" you ask the Captain.

"Demons," she says.

The pain crawls up the back of your head and you grab at the cabin as if wanting to take it off. All of your eyes closed tight.

White Rabbit cranks down the anchor and lowers you to the

floor.

"What's wrong?" she asks.

"It feels like a million spiders are crawling inside my head," you say.

You hear her flesh go tense under the vinyl catsuit.

"Is the pain coming from the bottom of the cabin?" she asks.

"Yes," you respond. "but it is moving up the back of my neck."

"Look through all of your eyes," the Captain raises you to your feet and stares at you with a stern white face. "Try to find where the spidery feelings are coming from."

You open your ship's eyes and see dozens of creatures berserking through the lower levels of the ship. They are like black demons. You see the people you left back in the cafeteria fighting them, but the creatures are too many. They cut Tendon down and open up Pussy Rot's stomach with their claws and scatter her insides around the room. The two faerie girls put up a good fight, but they are soon overtaken, their pretty butterfly wings shredded like paper.

"Some kind of creatures," you say. "Killing everyone. I think the Zhotrax got on board somehow."

"No," White Rabbit says. "It must be the dead."

"The dead?" you ask.

She grabs you by the arm and pulls you out of the room.

"Zombies," the Captain yells to you. "The ship is infested with zombies. The cannon fire must have woken them up."

You are racing down the hallway to the stairwell.

"Watch them through your eyes," she says. "Tell me when they get close."

You watch the undead thrashing through the hallways. Frog Girl is dangling from the ceiling as they eat her lower legs. You can see her screaming, but you don't hear anything.

The zombies are now just one floor away.

The high-pitched screams of the undead sound like twisting bone and bubbling plastic when White Rabbit takes you into the stair-well. You see Lox with a large axe just a dozen steps down, hacking away at shriveled black claws reaching desperately for his greasy flesh. But the walrus/man holds his ground, making sure the undead don't get any higher. His blubber ripples when he swings the axe.

On the top floor, you meet Eggy Joe and Studio under the landscape of eyes.

"Where are the others?" the Captain asks them.

Eve, White Rabbit's first lieutenant, steps out of the office with a box of guns and responds, "We haven't seen anyone else."

"They're all dead," you tell them. "Just us, and Lox in the stairwell."

But Lox is losing his balance. His breaths are heavy and he hardly has the energy to swing the axe anymore.

Eggy Joe breaks open the box of guns to find mostly old worn-out relics.

"What are these?" Joe asks the Captain. "They're shit."

"They aren't meant to be weapons," White Rabbit says. "They are antiques. And worth a fortune."

Eggy Joe and Studio dig through the pile of pistols, loading the ones that work.

"Get this stuff into the office," the Captain says. "We need to barricade ourselves in."

Eggy Joe raises his scrawny chest at the Captain.

"Fuck that," he says, with a finger in her face. "I'm not locking myself in there. We need to get to the lifeboats."

"We'll never make it to the lifeboats," the Captain says.

Eggy Joe squirts fluid from his elbow. "I'd rather die trying."

"Fine, you go. But the guns stay here."

Eggy Joe and Studio raise their weapons at the Captain and her lieutenant.

"No," he says. "The guns are coming with me."

"We'll vote then," the Captain says, to prevent the mutiny. "If the majority of us want to go, I'll agree to it." She looks at the faerie woman. "Eve, what do you think?"

Eve's eyes are rolling back like a shark's. "I say we stay."

"Two to two," White Rabbit says. "And now the tiebreaker

. . ."

Everyone stares at you, waiting for your vote.

If you vote to go for the lifeboats, turn to page 129.
If you vote to stay barricaded inside of the office, turn to page 137.

You go down with the ship like an idiot. Lard rushes into your lungs. It takes about three minutes for you to lose consciousness and three additional minutes for you to die.

You remain at the bottom of the ocean for ages.

Then—six thousand years after the fall of man—your fat-preserved remains are discovered by a team of telepathic, floating walrus heads. They intend to place your body in a museum, but wind up eating you as rations run low.

THE END

Salvatore/Timmy may be violent, but at least you don't have proof he's a killer.

You make a break for it.

"I expect ye back in the mess-hall toot-sweet!" Piratebeard calls out. "Got something special for ye to dance with!"

You barely hear him over the pounding of your feet and the thudding of your heart. On the way down, the flight of stairs had seemed impossibly long. Now, endorphins rush in torrents. Only seconds seem to pass before you reach the top.

On deck, Salvatore/Timmy still paces back and forth. You steel yourself and walk up to him.

"Uh, Salvatore/Timmy, sir?"

He looks at you, jaw set. "What the fuck do yah want?"

"I—I decided to help you overthrow Piratebeard."

His eyes light up; his Bronx accent vanishes. "Really, me boy. *Really!*"

You wonder if you spoke too soon.

"Uh, how long have you been here?"

"*Here?*"

"On this ship, I mean."

"About four days, give or take. Yeah, that sounds right, 'cause I got off *The Eye World* a week ago."

You sigh. The cabin boy had come aboard *after* the murder of the first crew. "Okay, that's all I needed to know. Now tell me what I can do to help *because the captain has bodies in the bilge.*"

Salvatore/Timmy removes a cylindrical metal object from his pocket. It bristles with knobs and wires. You find it odd that a cabin boy would have something so high-tech.

"What is it?"

He waves you off. "No time for questions. Just slip it onto yer little thingie and—"

"*My little thingie!*"

Salvatore/Timmy looks down. "Well it is a little thingie, now isn't it?"

You wilt. The cabin boy continues.

"Don't think I didn't see ye dancing like a girly harlot for those bastards. And, if they have their way, ye'll be dancing for them until the day ye die. *Dancing and more.*"

"But how will that help!" You point to the metal thing.

Salvatore/Timmy smiles. "When the captain reaches into yer drawers – and he will reach, I assure ye—he'll get a 100,000 volt surprise."

"But what about me! Won't it shock—"

"Nope, just as long as ye don't get it wet."

"Okay." You draw in deep breaths. "Let's do this."

"Shall I put it on for ye?"

You shake your head back and forth until it hurts. "No, please no! I can do it myself!"

Salvatore/Timmy backs away. He hands you the device with a warning: "Only touch these rubber pads. Touch anywhere else and yer dead."

Feeling very uncomfortable, you reach past the elastic waistband of your briefs. The thing slides on easily enough and creates a somewhat pleasurable tingling sensation.

The cabin boy regards you with a smile. "Now go, dance for Captain Partypants. Give 'em a show he'll never forget!"

Turn to page 109.

"No, Captain Piratebeard! Stop!"

The captain pulls away. Your elastic waistband snaps back hard.

"No one interrupts the footdance! 'Tis an affront to Merdelan!" His teeth clench. "Ye're a hot piece of man flesh, but—by golly—to the plank with ye!"

"You don't understand. There's a plot against—"

Piratebeard rears up and unsheathes his sword. He presses it into your back. "Oh, I understand perfectly! Guess the cabin boy will have to be our new kissyman."

"But the cabin boy is the one—"

"Shut yer hole!"

"Please!"

"No more lip flappin'! Get that sweet patooty outside and walk the plank!"

The captain won't relent. He jabs at your back, harder and harder, until you're standing on a thin board overlooking the sea of lard.

"Now jump, kissyman! *Jump!*"

You turn around. The cabin boy stares at you, glaring angrily. You expect no help from him.

"Please, Captain! I was only trying to help!"

His face turns red. "If ye really wanted to help then ye'd let me grope yer willy!"

The captain pushes you with all his might. You tumble, head over heels, into the sea of lard.

The place you fall isn't very deep; the ship is still in the harbor after all. You could have swum to shore if it wasn't for the electro-thing around your penis. As soon as the lard touches it, 100,000 volts of electricity surge through your shaft, killing you instantly.

Assorted tiny sea creatures soon copulate inside your skull.

THE END

"I say we go for the lifeboats," you say, and Eggy Joe smiles pointy teeth at the Captain.

White Rabbit gives you a dirty look and says, "Fine, let's go."

She goes to her office and grabs a stack of swords. She gives one to you, but you know you'll never be able to fight with the enormous box on your head.

"We need to get down two flights of stairs and through a very long hallway, all completely overrun with the undead," the Captain says. "We're going to have to fight our way through."

She taps Eggy Joe's peg leg with her toe and says, "Good luck."

You go down the stairwell and run into Lox still swinging his axe at the zombies, ready to collapse.

"We're going through them," White Rabbit tells the walrus man. "Forward!"

Lox nods his blubbery head and fixes his posture. Then plunges into the crowd of thrashing hands. You follow close behind the behemoth man as he rolls through the shrieking corpses, using him as your shield and only using your sword to push back the undead who slip under Lox's armpits. The others are right behind, shooting and hacking at the undead.

You go for several feet and then Lox stops. There aren't anymore zombies ahead of him. He looks back. You look back. The others are no longer behind you. They are still back there, fighting the spidery creatures. You don't see Eve or Studio at all. They must be buried in the crowd. Eggy Joe is struggling to free himself from black claws as rotten mouths take bites out of his neck and shoulders. His whines become high-pitched. And White Rabbit is laughing at him, happy he isn't going to make it..

The Captain cuts herself free of the crowd and heads toward you when there's a gunshot. A red hole opens up between her breasts. Blood trickles down her white vinyl as she looks down to see the bullet sticking halfway out of her chest. She pulls it out and examines it. Then turns to Joe with her tattooed eyebrows raised before collapsing to the floor.

"Let's go," Lox says, pulling you toward a hatch. "They're dead."

Turn to page 148.

You shake off your nerves and climb onto the log/bridge, stepping carefully across, with the pudgy Pussy Rot on your tail. She doesn't bother waiting her turn and crosses at the same time as you.

Looking down: the swirling of goopy fetuses makes you dizzy. You try concentrating on the bridge, but the giant vagina in the corner of your eyes keeps spewing out squiggly meat that is hard to ignore.

The log makes a crackling noise. There must be too much weight. But before you can tell Pussy Rot to go back, a mouth opens up beneath her and swallows her up to her armpits.

"A trap!" you scream.

The wooden mouth bites through the obese pirate's ribcage making a twisty-popping noise. And you see other mouths on the log in front of you and behind you. Their lips closed, but ready to snap open if you get too close.

Saryn flies at you and wraps you against her. She watches as Pussy Rot's corpse is slowly crunched and chewed, sinking downwards into the log's mouth.

"That's the third trap," Saryn says to the Captain as she brings you to safety. "There's only supposed to be three traps. That's the last one."

You watch as the last of Pussy Rot disappears into the wooden mouth, and the log becomes a regular log again.

"Perhaps," White Rabbit says. "The legend might be wrong."

"The bees, the forest, the bridge," Saryn has a bright smile. "That's three."

The Captain shrugs and continues on.

At the edge of the island's inner labia:

There is a path going into the vagina/cave alongside the river of fetus. The Captain sends Tendon in first to make sure it is safe. When he comes back, the lofty man just stands there, disinterested. His face is as bland as ever.

"Is it in there?" White Rabbit asks.

The stick man nods.

132

You enter, but it's too dark to see anything. The others don't seem to have a problem seeing in the dark, but you are walking blind.

If you want to wait outside the entrance, turn to page 113.
If you want to continue to walk blindly through the dark, turn to page 150.

Captain Piratebeard opens the sleeping chamber's door. He points you to your cot. After bidding him an awkward 'goodnight', you enter the room.

Your face turns into a scowl. Everything here is dark and musty. The only light comes from a saucer-sized portal. A host of randomly positioned bunks dot the floor. Some are ordered in straight rows. Others are in circle or zigzag formations. There must be a hundred of them, and each unit is stacked three beds high.

The room is mostly unoccupied. A handful of pirates are there, but all appear either asleep or dead. You tiptoe to your straw-filled cot. The last thing you want is to wake someone up.

A rat glares from atop your pillow. It nibbles on something that looks like a human ear. Cartilage crunches. The sound is nauseating. But the ear soon disagrees with the rat. It begins to spasm, belly hitching as yellow goopy stuff runs from its mouth onto your bed.

You've never seen anything quite so vile—and you've seen *lots* of disgusting things.

Grabbing the pillow, you toss both it and the rodent across the room. You remove your feces-filled jacket. It will never be worn again. Feeling infinitely cleaner, you lay on the cot, making sure your feet and not your head touch the rat-contaminated end.

Not that it makes a difference. No part of the bed feels safe. The straw isn't straw but freeze-dried worms. Large bugs coil through the nest. So many different colors: green, orange, blue—chartreuse even. So many different shapes: round, square, oblong—one's spiral. All, however, have hinged jaws, mean looking teeth, and blinking red eyes. Further back, a strange creature sits on haunches. It picks at its hair just inches from your head. The thing is the size of five thimbles and looks like a cross between a pickle and a shriveled monkey.

Its eyes flash blue.

You jump from the bunk before whatever it is notices you. The decision to sleep on the floor isn't a hard one to make.

Body pressed to the boards, you feel a rumbling. It's as though some large piece of equipment sits just underneath the floor. You're confused as to why a machine of any sort should be aboard a pirate ship, but the sensation is soothing. The gentle quakes vibrate your member, but not enough to give a distracting hard-on. Thoughts of rats, dead worms, and bugs with flashing eyes flee your mind. Your lids grow heavy and, in minutes, you're dead to the world.

Something's on your shoulder. You awake with a start. Whether hours or minutes have passed, you cannot say. Fog encircles your brain. For a second, you imagine you're back in Wyoming, back in your single-room apartment. You reach for the porn mag you keep on the nightstand. It's the only thing that gets you up in the morning. Then you see the other bunks. Then you smell the other pirates.

You recoil, boxing at the air in an attempt to ward off whatever touched you.

"Hold on there, me boy. I mean no harm."

The voice sounds familiar.

"Almost gave me a black eye, ye did." The man moves in closer. You breathe a sigh of relief. It's the cabin boy, Salvatore/Timmy.

"Sorry," you say, "I got startled."

"Worry not. 'Tis okay. Shouldn't have crept up like that."

"No problem." Your eyes dart around. "But what's happening? Anything wrong?"

"Nothing's happening. And nothing's wrong." Salvatore/Timmy smiles. "But it looks like ye rolled outta bed. Can't be comfortable down there."

The last thing you want this man to know is that you're scared of bugs and pickle/monkey things.

"Yeah, that's it. I rolled out of bed."

"It happens to the best of us. But that's not the reason I woke ye."

"Then why?"

Salvatore/Timmy arises. "I'll answer by showing ye. Let's go out on deck."

"Isn't it late?"

He unleashes another grin. "Late is the only time we have for

this, me boy."

"But what is *this*."

"Don't want to spoil the surprise."

Salvatore/Timmy's vagueness worries you. The man sees the concern in your eyes and puts his hand on your shoulder.

"I bet you be thinking that it's all work and no play here. Well, that ain't the case. I just want to show ye how us sea-farin' types get our kicks."

"But—"

He waves you off. "No buts. 'Tis perfectly harmless fun, so get up and join us on deck."

If you follow the cabin boy, turn to page 14.
If you choose to go back to bed, turn to page 58.

"I say we stay here," you tell them.

Eggy Joe says, "Son of a bitch!"

And he fires his antique pistol into your stomach, knocking you to the floor.

White Rabbit drives her electric claw into Joe's neck before he can fire another shot. Her fingers spread apart inside of him, electric jolts making his head jerk.

Studio fires his guns into Eve until he gets her in the head. Then turns to the Captain and continues firing. She uses Eggy Joe as her shield. When Studio runs out of bullets, she grabs Joe by the gun in his hand and twists his arm the wrong way, cracking bones, and pulls the trigger. Just one bullet to Studio's chest and the wheeler goes down.

Tossing Eggy Joe's corpse out of the way, White Rabbit sighs. She paces through the corpses kicking drops of blood into the air. Until she gets to you.

"Not dead?" she asks.

You shake your head.

"Let's get you inside," she says.

Before you can get to your feet, Lox explodes into the room screaming, "They're coming! They're coming!"

He wobbles across the eyeball landscape and helps the Captain take you into the office. They place you on the desk as they barricade the door.

"Where'd you get the hammer and nails?" you hear yourself saying. You feel as if you are drunk and can't control your words.

"This is where we hold up whenever there's a mutiny," she tells you, busy hammering boards across the wall. "We have all the supplies we'll need up in my bedroom."

A black claw breaks through the wall and grabs at White Rabbit's vinyl arm.

"Fucking cunts!" she screams, hammering the hand back into the wall. "This isn't going to work. Let's get into my bedroom."

The Captain slips off her white catsuit and pulls off her eyepatch. Then she opens her locker door and pulls herself up inside of it.

"Cabin Boy next," she says.

Lox picks you up off the desk and throws you over his shoulder, not gentle in the slightest. He shoves you into the locker and pushes on your butt until you are up inside. The Captain takes off your clothes and rubs grease on your body and then rubs her body against you until you are both nice and slippery.

She looks down the shaft into the locker to see Lox staring back at her.

"Come on, come on," she tells him. "What's holding you?"

"I'm too fat," he says. "I won't fit in there."

"Of course you'll fit. Just grease yourself up."

She hands him the can of lube.

"That's not going to help. I'm more than twice the size of this locker."

She squeezes his hand.

"I'll hold them off," he says and the Captain nods at him.

He closes the locker door and you hear him move the desk in front of it.

She turns to you. It is mostly dark. The only light is the sparks that come from the Captain's eyehole no longer covered by the eyepatch.

"Let's go," she says.

You go into a very thin crawlspace, just tall enough for you to fit lying down. And you have to pull yourself through with handles on the side of the wall, sliding your greasy naked skin against cold metal.

The enormous cube on your head makes shrilling noises as it scrapes across the metal of the shaft. Your stomach feels like acid and you begin to shiver. The shock is starting to wear off and the pain is coming in.

You are no longer moving. White Rabbit has to pull you by your head the rest of the way. Once you get into the room, too dark to see anything, you feel like your guts are going to pour out onto the floor at any second. She puts you in what you think is her bed, into her lap, and wraps her arms and legs around you. Pressing her slippery breasts against your back.

"Don't die, cabin boy," she says, rocking you in her arms. "I need you. Don't die."

"What are we supposed to do now?" the words cough out of you.

"We wait until the dead go back into hibernation," she says. "It shouldn't take longer than a week. We have all the food we need here. You can steer the ship in this room and take us to the nearest island or harbor. Then we can escape."

"What about the bullet in my stomach?" you ask. "Am I going to—"

A sharp pain in your head cuts you off. You cry out. Then another sharp pain, and another, coming from somewhere inside the cube on your head. You open the ship's eyes and see the undead coming at you.

"What's wrong?" White Rabbit asks.

"They're eating the eyes out of the walls," you say.

And you scream again, as claws dig into more ship eyes just outside the office door.

The pain continues for several hours. The Captain holds you and hums to you in a sweet voice, combing the blood out of your pubic hair. Your body is all numb and your muscles won't move anymore.

She stops humming and your consciousness drifts away to the sound of electric currents flowing through her head.

THE END

"I think you should retire," you say.

And a big smile opens up on the White Rabbit's face.

"You're right, I should," she says. "Now we can get married and have kids and live happily ever after."

Your face is in a kind of twitchy freeze when she runs off to the orgy screaming, "We're getting married! The Cabin Boy and me! Married!" Then she goes back to having sex with them.

You get married on the ship. You in a tuxedo with the enormous electric cube attached to your skull. The Captain with her bald head and eyepatch and white wedding gown.

Years pass.

White Rabbit becomes pregnant and has a litter of electronic babies. Ten of them. And then she gets pregnant again. And again. Until the ship is swarming with little bald children with static voices. They don't seem to like the idea that you're their father. They prefer the company of their aunt Saryn or uncle Tendon.

The ship is anchored and doesn't go anywhere. Nobody cares about adventuring. They are more interested in relaxing and playing with the children. There is a large farm on the roof of the Eye World and Saryn eats the fetuses out of the sea. You haven't been eating much, so you are getting bony and weak.

White Rabbit stops fucking you and so you have an affair with Trapface. She isn't the best company, and her face gives you nightmares, but she is the most comfortable to be around. The warmest body to curl up to.

Once the children are grown men and women, you are forgotten about entirely. There is a new society in the Eye World with White Rabbit as the matriarch, Saryn as patriarch. And you'd prefer to have nothing to do with them.

You disappear into the lower levels of the ship and become a ghost. Your children's children tell stories about you that keep them awake at night. Sometimes you will weigh anchor and move the ship around to give them a scare. Sometimes you consider driving the ship into the ocean.

Eventually, you run into the undead who live in rooms behind the dungeon. You want them to end your life, as violently as they can. But instead of killing you they take you in and make you one of their own.

The rest of your days are spent drifting between life and death, losing all senses and dreaming about worlds far away. You outlive most of your children, and your children's children, until your bones crumble to dust.

THE END

You're a sick fuck.

THE END

Lox is the first to volunteer, raising his flabby walrus arm. Then Frog Girl and Eggy Joe. And just before Studio can raise his wheeled hand to join his leaky partner on the mission, your arm darts into the air.

"Cabin boy?" White Rabbit asks. "You can't go out there, we need you with the ship."

Said, who is shaving her head bald with a straight razor, perhaps her way of mourning her dead sister, says to the Captain, "No, I think he should go. His ship's eyes will have a unique view of the entire island. We'll be able to reach the womb more easily."

The Captain nods her head. "Okay, he will go with you. But protect the cabin with your life. If he dies, remove his head and bring it back."

The lieutenants agree and you get ready for the mission while waiting for the metal bees to die away.

Your equipment consists of several bags for carrying treasure and that's it. You don't get any weapons. The others get swords and guns. Lox has some kind of laser gun, which he poses with in the mirror to pretend he's some kind of deformed-blob-of-blubber-in-bondage-straps version of Buck Rogers, or maybe a character from Aeon Flux.

They take you down to the loading deck that opens up to the fetus ocean like a garage door. The meaty smell of the ocean fills the room, like menstrual blood mixed with raw beef. You board a long rowboat and the remaining lieutenant, Saryn, lowers it into the embryonic soup.

The smell is stronger once the boat splatters into the muck. But it is not the dead and rotting flesh smell that you might have expected. The fetuses in the ocean do not even seem to be dead. They seem to be breathing. Some of them kick or roll. Like they are still inside of their wombs. Perhaps the entire ocean is their womb.

You hit the beach and wade through fetus goop to pull the

boat ashore. The beach is very smooth and tan, with a texture like rubber.

"Which way looks easiest?" they ask you.

You look through your ship's eyes and see yourself on the beach. Examining the landscape, there doesn't seem to be an easy route.

"I don't see a trail or path," you say.

"What would be the safest?" Kumi asks.

"Or quickest," Said says.

You look carefully. "Perhaps if we traveled around the side to the thick jungle area and came at the vagina from the belly."

"No," Said says, rubbing her freshly shaved head. "Let's climb up it from the asshole. We don't want to go through the damn pubic hair."

Said starts walking before we agree, mumbling, "I hate pubic hair."

Kumi runs ahead and stops her sister.

"You stay here with the others," she tells her. "I'm going to see if you can climb it from that angle."

Kumi's black faerie wings flutter and lift her from the ground to the sky. From the ship's eyes, she looks like a moth drawn to the enormous vagina like a light. You notice Said's wings are more shredded than the others. You don't think she's able to fly like her sisters. She plops down next to you and puts her bald head in her hand.

Then she turns to you. "Okay, here's the plan," Said whispers. "I want you to weigh anchor and walk in place until The Eye World is far away. Too far for them to make it here by rowboat."

"What do you mean?" you ask.

"We're going to keep the treasure for ourselves. You want to be rich, don't you? The Captain is far too greedy to share her riches. We need to kill her before she kills us."

You stare at her, not sure what to say.

"I have it all planned out," she continues. "Saryn, my sister still on board, will kill the Captain and take command of the ship. You will be able to see if she succeeds or fails through the ship's eyes. If she succeeds you can bring the ship back to the island to pick us up. If she fails you can leave the ship out there until the Captain starves to death. Eggy Joe is with us and Frog Girl won't oppose us, but we might have to kill Lox. He is very loyal to White Rabbit. My sister, Kumi, might also oppose us, but I doubt she'll actually fight us now that Eve is dead. She doesn't know how to think without her older sister around."

"I don't want to die," you find yourself saying. Not at all sure how or why you said it.

The demon girl snickers at you, rolling her dead white eyes.

The other crew members are squirming against the plastic beach next to you, but they didn't seem to have heard Said's conversation. You hope Lox did not hear. His laser gun, or whatever it is, sure looks like it could kill everyone around him in an instant.

It's been an hour and Kumi hasn't returned.

"She's dead," Said says.

"There's no question about it," Eggy Joe says.

"She must have sprung a trap, or maybe there's more of those electric bees around." Said doesn't sound very distressed, but she cuts lines into the back of her arm for some reason. "Let's go through the pubic hair."

You start hiking up the squeaky plastic mountain to the jungle of long green trees. Before too long, the group gets tired of trudging uphill. Lox is especially tired, gravel-breathing with his short fat tongue sticking out.

Said stands next to you and winks. Then looks back at Eggy Joe and winks at him, who jumps the walrus man from behind. Stabbing him with his dagger. And Said jumps him from the front, clawing his gun from his hand.

Frog Girl run-hops away and you follow her. Into the forest. You crouch down behind some long hair-shaped trees, taking a peek back at the fight from a safe distance.

"What's going on?" Frog Girl asks with an innocent face. Like she's never heard of a mutiny before.

"They want to kill the Captain," you tell her. "And they're going to kill everyone loyal to her."

Lox is stabbed and clawed, over and over again, but he has too much fat for them to puncture any major organ. He squeals and flails around, bleeding, shoving at them and trying to run away. But they just keep coming back.

Frog Girl decides not to wait for the outcome and runs deeper into the jungle. You turn to follow, but before you can take a single step you feel a tingling sensation crawling up the back of your neck.

Then your head explodes.

THE END

You don't give the bastard a chance to touch you. You wait until it's within arm's reach. Wrapping you fingers around its slick, repulsive neck, you squeeze until the thing goes limp.

Letting go, you watch it slip beneath lard waves.

The shore is only a few feet away so you wade there. Pirate life just isn't for you.

You leave Pirate Town without incident, but are torn apart by green teeth in the neighboring city:

ZOMBIE TOWN.

THE END

The lifeboat is a patched together floatation device made of rubber and plates of metal. It is circular and has a small shelter big enough for three people or Lox to sleep in comfortably. Outside the shelter is a small yard with green tinsel for grass and two chests full of supplies. The boat should also have some kind of sail to go on the mast, but Lox can't find it anywhere.

You float on top of the lard for several days, trying to get to know the strange walrus/man who doesn't ever feel like talking to you. He might be the worst company you've ever known. And sometimes, when he's horny, he'll flip you on your back and rip apart your rectal cavity with his wrinkly bulbous cock. Sometimes he'll give you some drugs to knock you out before raping you, but other times he doesn't seem to care.

"How do I get this big metal box off of my head?" you ask the walrus/man.

"You don't," he grunts.

"But we aren't on the ship anymore," you say.

He slurps sardines from a can.

"It'll kill you," he says.

A few weeks go by.

Both of you are greasy and smelly and coated in flies. The entire ocean is coated in flies.

You don't bother talking to Lox anymore. You only communicate when he grunts at you to turn over and you grumble at him because you're out of drugs.

You cross paths with a fishing boat and the sailors stare at you bug-eyed as they see you dangling over the edge of the boat getting ass-raped by the enormous walrus/man. Lox makes chug-huffing noises as he fucks, his blubber shuffling and bouncing with each thrust. And by the expressions on their faces, they seem very sympathetic to the agony you are going through. Some of them even have tears in their eyes for you. One takes off his hat and presses it against his heart. Another pounds his fists against the railing like he promises to avenge you.

But in the end, they decide not to pick you up.

THE END

You walk aimlessly through the dark, your arms outstretched.

Trying to follow the sounds of their footsteps, you feel somebody's shoulder. You hold onto it, to be escorted. But the person jerks around at you. And just when you realize it is the girl, Trapface, your hand goes into her metal jaws and they clamp down with a whack.

You cry out, thrashing away from her, but the bear trap that she has instead of a face is digging deep into your flesh. You fall to your knees and shove your face into her chest to muffle the scream.

The Captain's fingers light up like bulbs, brightening the room.

Dark blood gushing down your arm when Trapface frees you from her head.

White Rabbit takes you by the hand through the darkness, leading you with glow-fingers.

"Come here," she says. "I have something to show you."

You squat down in a corner and the Captain reveals Pussycat's treasure: hundreds of gold-encrusted cocks.

"Are those dildos?" you ask.

"Not just dildos," she says, digging through the treasure chest next to her. "There are butt plugs, vibrators, anal sliders, Thai beads, pocket pussies, ass shakers, cock rings, everything you could hope for. Pussycat had all of her gold melted down and molded into a collection of sex toys. It's more beautiful than my dreams."

There is a glimmering in White Rabbit's eye. You think you see a tear.

"Come on," she says. "I want to try them out."

And your heart skips a beat when she raises a monster-sized jewel-encrusted dildo with a baby-sized fist for a head.

Back at the ship, the pirates throw an orgy party, fucking all of the gold.

You try to drink as much rum as you can so you won't feel the pain of your ripped asshole and the raw holes in your wrist. They try to entice you into their pit of sex, waving their greasy breasts at you, but you ignore them. They don't force you to fuck them yet.

The White Rabbit sits next to you on a bench, naked but wearing her eyepatch, drunk with sex and she falls against your shoulders.

"We got it," she says to you. "The treasure we always dreamed of."

She puts her bald head in your lap and stares up at you. "Perhaps I should retire."

Her eyes drift shut and there's a smile creeping her lips.

Then her eyes pop open. "What do you think?"

You stutter. "What do you mean?"

"Should we retire?" she asks. "Buy a mansion in the country, get married, live fancy quiet lives until we die. How does that sound?"

If you think White Rabbit should retire, turn to page 140.
If you think White Rabbit should remain a pirate, turn to page 170.

You've never been a brave person. You always back down or capitulate, even when it means the death of your entire race.

And today is no different.

"Yes, yes, whatever! Make me a robot! *Just don't hurt me!*"

A red diode blinks. "Your decision is wise. Come outside. We shall await the arrival of the *beep* mothership."

You follow *Kuntis Mechanus*. You realize he—if you can still call him *he*—no longer walks. Instead, he rolls about on shiny red wheels.

You ask, feeling awkward, "am I going to get a set of wheels, too?"

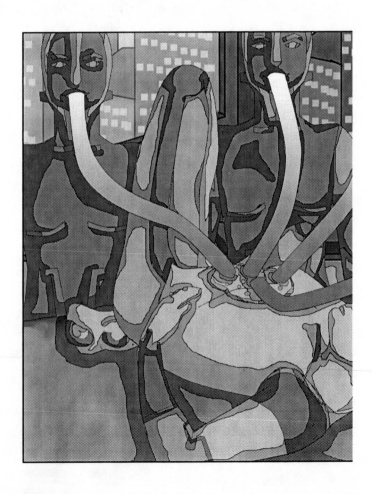

A box-like head turns to you. "Yes, you will have all the attributes I possess. You won't miss your *beep* human form. The pleasures in my world are ten-times anything you know."

"Really?"

"Let me *beep* show you." *Kuntis Mechanus* extends a throbbing wire from his midsection. "Put this in your mouth. See what I mean."

Your face blanches. "*You want to rape me, too!*"

"Get your mind out of the *beep* gutter. This is an experience-transfer unit. Please accept my offering."

Feeling awkward for the seven millionth time, you slip the cord into your mouth.

Your vision explodes in shards. A whirling wire-encrusted vista opens behind your eyes. You find yourself in a high-tech geodesic penthouse. Outside, conical skyscrapers rise from a silver street on which insect-like vehicles travel. Inside, she-bots writhe on silken blankets. You recline beside them, in new mechanized form. Hundreds of steel and plastic protuberances extend from your body. The she-bots take them into their mouths and make whirling sounds. The sensation is like birth, sex, and death all rolled up in one glistening package.

Kuntis Mechanus retracts the cord back into his body.

"Hey," you frown. "I was just about to get my rocks off!"

"No time," the robot bleeps. "The Mothership is here."

You look up. Your mouth hangs in a rictus. A shimmering, doughnut-shaped craft hovers in the sky, making no sound. A beam of light shines down from a hole in its golden body. The ray envelops *The Rotten Sore*. Floorboards shake as wood splinters and folds in on itself. You cover your eyes. You fear the ship is about to sink – but the vessel is merely reforming. In seconds, *The Rotten Sore* has mutated into a towering, wire-strewn cube much like *The Eye World*. But the sight no longer repulses or unnerves you. In fact, you find it *cool*.

And you think you know why.

Your transformation has begun, too.

Hands morph into hinged steel knives. Arms become rods that branch from your galvanized steel frame. You laugh, but your voice comes out in bleeps.

Kuntis Mechanus takes you by your new hand and together you float up into the mothership for a quick debriefing.

Your new mission is one of human destruction and fevered robotic sex.

Hell yeah.

THE END

Piratebeard slams his fist against the mess hall's window. "Come all ye scallywags! Join us for the dance to end all dances!"

Pirates pour out of the room in droves. They follow their captain to the stern. You trail close behind.

A few minutes later, everyone stops in front of the ship's steering wheel. It looks like that of a sports car, only much bigger. There's even a horn in the center. You gawk at it, amazed.

"No time to admire the wheel!" Piratebeard shoves the golden baton into your hand. "'Tis the hour to dance *The Dance of Merdelan!*"

"I —I don't know *The Dance of Merdelan.*"

"Then follow me!" Piratebeard begins to bump and grind. Ass shimmying, hands flapping—his dance looks like a cross between *The Bump* and *The Hot Chocolate.*

You follow his steps to the best of your ability, shaking *The Scepter of Merdelan* when necessary.

Forty-five minutes pass. Piratebeard ends his dance, and you take this as your cue to stop. You fall against the steering wheel, exhausted.

"Now stand back," he says. "The dancing ritual is complete; the ship must set sail."

You slink away. Piratebeard removes a set of keys from his pocket and inserts one into the wheel's ignition.

"The ship has an engine!"

"Aye, souped up it is."

Piratebeard turns the keys. A motor revs. It's the same sound you heard under your sleeping quarters last night.

"But pirate ships don't have—"

Piratebeard stomps the gas pedal. Your words disintegrate as the ship takes off so quickly it gives you whiplash. You turn around. Only seconds into the voyage, and the people on the shore already look like ants.

Piratebeard cackles, waving his hands in the air. "Now let us all sing the sea chanty of sweet, sweet death!"

Your eyes bulge like grapes. "Sweet, sweet *what!*"

Piratebeard ignores you and begins the song. A few members of his crew mumble the lyrics. Others just scream.

Yo ho ho ho, we'll soon be dead as can be.
Yo ho ho ho, our bodies will fester and bloat in the sea.

You want to go cackle-cackle mad.

But Merdelan will protect us.
Aye, he'll be our guide.

You pull at your hair. You pull at your face.

He'll sheathe us in dark garments
with lots of young boys by his side.

Piratebeard stops singing and makes a proclamation, his tone no longer pirate-like: "After death, my astral form will be known by the holy name *Vordlak*. But, please, call me that now."

Your brain feels like it's melting. You imagine it drip, drip, dripping out your ears.

"And you shall all be servants." He points in your direction. "But you, my son, shall sit by Vordlak's right hand."

"But Captain Piratebeard—"

No! Call me *Vordlak*! And wait until I'm finished!" A gout of green fire explodes from his mouth. "*Okay!*"

You fall silent as bowels loosen.

"I have waited since I was 26 for this day to arrive. And now my heart shall spill its ashes into the sea. I shall unite with Merdelan as this ship unites with stone."

You look out across the stern. A monolithic rock rises from the sea of lard. Vordlak turns the wheel towards it. His crew cheers and farts.

But you don't cheer or fart. You're too scared to move.

The sound of someone running draws your attention. You turn and see Salvatore/Timmy. He pushes through the mass of stinking old pirates and jumps the man who used to be Piratebeard.

The cabin boy is much younger and stronger-looking than the captain, but Vordlak stands his ground. He doesn't even flinch. Salvatore/Timmy looks stunned.

"Could you please stop bothering me?"

The cabin boy punches him in the face.

"Don't say I didn't ask nicely." Red lasers shoot from both eyes. They penetrate the cabin boy's head, exploding it. Meaty shards rain down. The headless corpse falls away.

Vordlak wipes gunk off his jacket. He floors the gas pedal and shouts "*Full speed ahead*!"

The ship rockets through lard. Faster and faster and faster and faster. You reach for the side railing and wrap your arms and legs around it.

The impact is going to be huge.

"*Shiver me timbers*!" Vordlak's appendages flare like the plumage of the proudest peacock. "*And praise Merdelan*! *Praise Merdelan*! *Praise Merdelan*!"

The rock fills your vision. It looks bigger than Everest. Judging by what you see, the ship is going to side-strike the rock at an angle. You close your eyes, not wanting to see anymore.

A blast like a million tons of exploding TNT rings in your ear. Your brain feels jarred loose as your body slides violently across the railing. Wooden splinters that look more like sticks embed themselves in your arms and chest.

You open your eyes, expecting to be dead. But, if you are, hell is *The Rotten Sore*.

Awe and horror overtake you. The ship is in fragments. Three large pieces remain and, luckily, one of them is the stern.

But it's sinking fast.

You look around, still too stunned to move. The crew obviously hadn't held onto anything. All were knocked off on impact. It's just you and the captain now. And he's still standing by the wheel, a golden aura encasing his form.

"Ah shite! I'm not dead yet!"

Vordlak relinquishes his hold on the wheel and waits for the goopy white stuff to reach deck-level. Then he lies down, his golden aura quickly surrendering to the whiteness of lard.

He never resurfaces.

Fat rushes up to meet you. Perhaps you should just end it now. Perhaps you should stop fighting and go down with the ship. There's nothing going for you—just the prospect of jail and sodomy at the hands of people named Big Tom or Bubba.

But there isn't much time to decide.

The railing you cling to is going under.

If you go down with the ship, turn to page 124.
If you fight it out, turn to page 159.

There's no way in hell you're going down with the ship. You're too much of a coward to face death.

You break your hold on the railing, expecting to float up. Instead, you go in the opposite direction. The boat's sinking has created a terrible vortex. Further and further, you swirl down.

Something brushes against you—a large plank of wood. You take hold of it, grasping with both hands.

The suction won't relent. It pulls at both you and the board. Your lungs pulse, throb, and then ache. Drowning seems inevitable.

But the vortex ebbs once the ship sinks deeper and deeper into its eternal bed of fat. The board is buoyant and rises slowly to the surface, taking you with it.

Once above the waves, you greedily inhale salty/fatty air. The scent would have repulsed you only minutes earlier. Now, it smells like ambrosia. Some time passes before you can breathe normally again, your hand clutching the board, your feet treading lard.

You gaze up at the sun. It looks like a huge red eye that beats down unblinkingly on your red and salty face.

A meaty seagull lands on the plank. It waddles up to you, attempting to peck out your eyes. You swat at it, and the thing falls into patties.

Hours seem to pass. Finally, off in the distance, you see pristine sands and the swarthy/nasty pirates that mill along the beach. You never imagined you'd feel grateful to see such people.

But the ocean—it feels suddenly hotter. A bubble arises. Then another. It appears as though the lard is about to boil.

And now it's not only hot – it's *painful*.

You try to climb further atop the door, but the lard has made your body too slick. You keep sliding back into the hotter and hotter sea.

The door slides out of your grip. Agony won't let you keep hold. It floats away as you flail through rapidly bubbling fat.

"Help me!" You scream. "*Help me!*" But you're at least a hundred feet from the shore, and no one's going to be stupid enough to jump headlong into this boiling sea.

Your skin turns lobster red as your eyes go white. Your dead body puffs up once it's well done.

Meat falls from the bone once you're overcooked.

In a different dimension, a monolithic, belarded Merdelan turns up the heat on the frying pan containing the sea of lard. He places two grokfish steaks into the grease and proceeds to bang a hot merflid as the ocean boils away on his stove.

THE END

Out on deck, you run toward Salvatore/Timmy. You're in such a hurry that you almost run headlong into the comatose pirate rolling back and forth in his wheelchair.

You near the cabin boy. It seems as though he's just pacing back and forth. You stop behind him and grasp his shoulder. He jumps with a start, though the frown on his face soon melts into a smile.

"Ye startled me, but I guess that's only fair."

"Yes, but——"

Salvatore/Timmy grins. "And ye're looking a bit bare today, matey."

You cover the front of your underwear with your hand. You're embarrassed that Salvatore/Timmy—and everyone else for that matter – is seeing you in such a state. But he doesn't seem to mind. No hungry stares on his part. "Yeah, Piratebeard kinda lost my clothes."

"Aye, that sounds like Captain Dwarfsmasher, the swarthy whore."

You're taken aback. "Wait, I thought you liked Piratebeard."

Salvatore/Timmy spits angrily upon the deck. "Oh no, sir. I can't stand the bugger. Not a bit, I tell ye. Not a bit."

"That's surprising. But I can't say I like him much either."

"Remember last night when I wanted ye to go out and have some fun?"

You nod.

"Well, there was another reason, too. I couldn't say much—not then—not until I knew if ye were the right man to tell."

"Okay, but where are you going with this?"

Salvatore/Timmy looks around. "I'll lay it on the line, then. *I want yer help in overthrowing Captain Freaknasty.*"

"*What!*"

"His crew of old farts won't protect him. They don't know their asses from a walrus' ugly mug!"

"But——"

"It's got to be done. Captain Assplug must fall!"

Your brain swirls. The cabin boy was supposed to help, not

make things more complicated. "I don't know if that's the smartest thing to—"

The cabin boy's tone adopts a decided edge: "What say ye?"

You stutter. "I-I-I said I don't know."

His voice, now Bronx-accented and violent, rings in your ear:

"I don't know who the fuck yah think yah are, bitch. The queen? Is that who yah fuckin' think yah are? Shall I kiss yer royal feet? Will that please yer highness? Will that give yah a queenly hard-on?"

You back so tightly against the wall that your flesh feels fused to the boards.

Foam flies from the cabin boy's mouth. "Know what I'll do if yah say no? Do yah, cunt? Do yah!"

"No," you mumble. "I have no idea. Please, please just let me—"

"Okay then, I'll tell yah. I'll fuck yah and fuck yah wife and fuck yah kids whether yah got 'em or not." Salvatore/Timmy reaches into his trousers and pulls out a grossly oversized cock. He waves it around a bit. "And I'll lay it to 'em with this here chunk o'meat."

You unleash a girlish scream. Nothing seems real anymore. It feels like everything you've ever known is crumbling to dust.

If you've had enough and lose it all, turn to page 30.
If you run back to Piratebeard, turn to page 27.

You're not in the best of shape. Ordinarily, even the most trivial exercise gets you winded. Now, however, you climb the rope without reservation. Your muscles feel big as you pull yourself up and up and up.

If only merflids were around during high-school gym class. . .

But the past no longer concerns you. You're a changed man. You don't even feel the desire to molest children. It's as though your body and soul have been sponged clean.

You near the top. You can't wait to thank Salvatore/Timmy for pushing you over the edge into this beautiful sea full of beautiful creatures. You reach for the gunwall and crane your neck to see over it.

You gasp. Salvatore/Timmy isn't there.

But the old man in the wheelchair is. And Captain Piratebeard, too.

He looks pissed.

"Captain?" you say.

He walks over to you. "Don't ye know only the captain dances with merflids!"

You shake your head. "No, I just went out with—"

"This is a pirate ship, and on pirate ships we have rules. *Cardinal* rules. Rules of the sea."

"I know, but—"

"Break these rules, and ye must be reprimanded."

You pull yourself up, gibbering. "But I didn't mean anything by it! Really!"

"Ye have a fine way of wishing yer captain happy birthday."

Buoyant enlightenment fades, leaving heavy dread. "I didn't know I was breaking any rules! *Honest*!"

Piratebeard's face softens. "I know, me boy. And I don't mind much. Other captains might keelhaul ye on sight, but I think of meself as an enlightened scallywag."

"So, what are you going to do?"

"Not sure." Captain Piratebeard removes a tattered paperback from his coat pocket. "Let me check the handbook."

You see the title in raised blue lettering:

YE OLDE PIRATE CAPT'N HANDBOOK

Captain Piratebeard looks up from the pages. "Sorry to keep ye waitin', matey. I'm not as young as I used to be. I tell ye, the walrus remembers better than me these days."

You watch, waiting for Piratebeard to find the right section. He leafs through pages, going from one end of the book to the other.

"I know it's here somewhere. Ah, here it is!" Piratebeard brings a pair of reading glasses to his eyes. "On page 165."

Anxiety grips you. "So, what does it say?"

Piratebeard looks up. "It's not too bad, me boy. Just decapitation. That's all."

Turn to page 62.

Waxing nonchalant is hard when you're standing amongst a hundred or more corpses, but you give it a shot.

"I —I understand perfectly, Mr. Captain Piratebeard, sir."

He arches his brows. "Ye do?"

"Oh yes. Yes, sir. A man of adventure can't stay put. He has to . . . do stuff."

"Aye, ye be speakin' truth, me boy!"

"And the old crew. I'm sure they were . . . ummm . . . bad pirates."

Piratebeard shakes his head. "Good for killin' and little else."

"Yeah. Yeah, that's right. You made a good decision – to murder those guys and all."

"True, me boy. But there's no use dwellin' on past adventures when there's dancin' to be done." He fishes around the nest of corpses and withdraws a golden baton. Pink plastic streamers hang down from the shaft. "I stashed this here because certain members of me crew are attracted to shiny things."

"What is it?"

"It be *The Holy Scepter of Merdelan*. 'Tis a supreme honor for ye to dance and rub yerself with this!"

The smile on your face burns like acid. "I'll gladly rub myself with something so priceless."

"That's a good boy." His voice suddenly adopts a fevered cadence. "But we must hurry on deck so ye can dance yer final dance!"

Final dance?

"We've already dillydallied too long; the hour is nigh!"

You don't have time to question this. Piratebeard grabs your arm and sprints through the hallway. You're winded by the time you reach the base of the stairs, but Piratebeard presses on. You're amazed his old heart hasn't exploded.

In fact, you're amazed *your* heart hasn't exploded. By what feels like the five millionth step, that organ is breaking out of its cage. You close your eyes and allow Piratebeard to lead you upwards. Maybe time will pass by quicker if you don't have to see that still-tiny pinprick of light.

Finally, the captain stops. You collapse on the deck, bathed in sweat, huffing and puffing. Piratebeard glowers down at you, perfectly composed.

"No time for rest, me boy. Ye must dance *The Dance of Merdelan!*"

Turn to page 155.

You call out to the flying woman, but she is too far up in the air. You scream with all your breath, but she does not hear you. She disappears into the horizon.

Looking in all directions, there is nothing. Just the blobbing white sea. The warmth of the ooze is intense. Like boiling tar. It heats up your blood and makes you go dizzy. Your eyes rolling into the back of your head . . .

You go in and out of consciousness. Not sure what is happening to you. At one point you are removed from the sea and put on some kind of enormous raft. It is the size of a small island, made of logs tied together, a floating village.

When you find your senses, you are surrounded by skinny wooden people with windmills for heads. They are on all sides of you, standing like statues and cocking their necks. Speaking in whooshing noises instead of in words.

They just stare at you. And you back at them.

You continue like this for almost an hour.

Until the wind dies down and the wooden people go to sleep.

THE END

"Don't retire," you tell the White Rabbit.

She wrinkles up one side of her face and gives it a thought.

"Yeeeeah," she says. "I was born to be a pirate. That's the life for me."

So you go on to seek adventure on the ocean of animal fetuses. But before you find a single ship to attack and molest, you're swept up in another whirlpool and transported to yet another ocean. This time the ocean is made of twentieth century apartment buildings and The Eye World becomes jammed between two of them. So you and the rest of the crew abandon ship and move into one of the apartments in the ocean of apartment buildings. The rent isn't too bad, but it's been difficult adjusting to the natural food chain in this ocean. There are smaller people walking around that you have to catch for food. And you have to watch out for the bigger people that want to eat you.

Saryn has you naked between her knees as she tattoos dragon scales on your back. Outside your window, large hooks are hanging down from somewhere beyond the pink clouds. You close your eyes and relax with the gentle swaying of the apartment building, breathing in the salt from the couch. You believe you're beginning to like it here. If you could only remove the big pointless cabin from your head . . .

THE END

You eat the diaper's contents for three days of living hell before developing thirty-four different diseases.

Twenty-one of the thirty-four prove fatal.

Five are totally unknown to medical science.

THE END

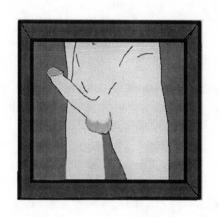

BIOS

Carlton Mellick III is the author 9 books of surreal satire and the dark bizarre, such as RAZOR WIRE PUBIC HAIR, FISHY-FLESHED, THE MENSTRUATING MALL, THE BABY JESUS BUTT PLUG, and SATAN BURGER, which has been the #1 best-selling horror novel at amazon.com for at least 5 seconds. He has sold 80 short stories to magazines and anthologies, including THE YEAR'S BEST FANTASY AND HORROR 16.

Visit him online at www.avantpunk.com

Kevin L. Donihe is the world's oldest living wombat. When not doing other things, he tends to write erotic books about walruses. His novel, SHALL WE GATHER AT THE GARDEN?, was released in 2001 by Eraserhead Press. The same press will release his THE FLAPPY PARTS soon. Kevin's short fiction has appeared in over 140 publications in ten countries. Venues include THE MAMMOTH BOOK OF LEGAL THRILLERS, FLESH & BLOOD, CHIAR-OSCURO, THE CAFE IRREAL, POE'S PROGENY, SICK: AN ANTHOLOGY OF ILNESS, and others. He also edits BARE BONE for Raw Dog Screaming Press, a story from which was re-printed in THE MAMMOTH BOOK OF BEST NEW HORROR 13.

Kevin lives somewhere. Do not attempt to visit him. That would be a bad mistake.

Just visit his website at: http://users.chartertn.net/mbs/kldwriter

Terrasa Ulm sleeps under a blanket of stars with her Toad and her Boolean. She passes the time programming utterly inane games, creating art in many forms, being an absent-minded professor, and adventuring on the high seas and the low roads. If she were less imaginary, perhaps she would avoid sharing her life online at www.siamesequbits.com.

ERASERHEAD PRESS

www.eraserheadpress.com

Books of the surreal,
absurd, and utterly
strange

WWW.AVANTPUNK.COM
A New Imprint From Eraserhead Press

BIZARRE NOVELS BY
CARLTON MELLICK III

RAZOR WIRE PUBIC HAIR * STEEL BREAKFAST ERA
BABY JESUS BUTT PLUG * ELECTRIC JESUS CORPSE
SATAN BURGER * THE MENSTRUATING MALL
TEETH AND TONGUE LANDSCAPE * FISHY-FLESHED

Printed in the United States
100998LV00002B/287/A